SPECIAL MESSAGE TO READERS

This book is published under the auspices of
THE ULVERSCROFT FOUNDATION
(registered charity No. 264873 UK)

Established in 1972 to provide funds for
research, diagnosis and treatment of eye diseases.
Examples of contributions made are: —

A new Children's Assessment Unit at
Moorfield's Hospital, London.

Twin operating theatres at the
Western Ophthalmic Hospital, London.

A Chair of Ophthalmology at the
University of Leicester.

The establishment of a Royal Australian College
of Ophthalmologists "Fellowship".

You can help further the work of the Foundation
by making a donation or leaving a legacy. Every
contribution, no matter how small, is received
with gratitude. Please write for details to:

**THE ULVERSCROFT FOUNDATION,
The Green, Bradgate Road, Anstey,
Leicester LE7 7FU, England.
Telephone: (0116) 236 4325**

**In Australia write to:
THE ULVERSCROFT FOUNDATION,
c/o The Royal Australian College of
Ophthalmologists,
27, Commonwealth Street, Sydney,
N.S.W. 2010.**

5 BULLETS FOR JUDGE BLAKE

While the escapees were headed for Alvison, Wyoming, bent on wreaking bloody vengeance on the crippled judge who sentenced them, two Texas trouble-shooters drifted into that town and ran foul of the law and the local sharpers. They also found new friends, the kind deserving of their protection. When the chips were down, it would be Larry and Stretch versus the killer-pack.

MARSHALL GROVER

5 BULLETS
FOR
JUDGE BLAKE

A Larry & Stretch Western

Complete and Unabridged

LINFORD
Leicester

First published in Australia in 1981 by
Horwitz Grahame Books Pty Limited
Australia

First Linford Edition
published 1996
by arrangement with
Horwitz Publications Pty Limited
Australia

British Library CIP Data

Grover, Marshall
   Larry & Stretch: 5 bullets for Judge Blake.
   —Large print ed.—
   Linford western library
   1. Australian fiction—20th century
   I. Title
   823 [F]

   ISBN 0–7089–7910–6

Published by
F. A. Thorpe (Publishing) Ltd.
Anstey, Leicestershire
Set by Words & Graphics Ltd.
Anstey, Leicestershire
Printed and bound in Great Britain by
T. J. Press (Padstow) Ltd., Padstow, Cornwall

This book is printed on acid-free paper

1

The Bormann Breakout

IT was to be one of the darkest days in the history of the Wyoming Territory. The mettle of law officers, local and Federal, would be put to the test and the territory's prison system overhauled, security tightened, boards of enquiry set up and the frontier press spreading the story far and wide.

The evil architect of the big breakout, Number 679, Cole Alton, was lean, cold-eyed and thick-bearded, a lifer of predatory and murderous instincts. At 10 o'clock of that memorable morning, he was in the exercise yard with 70 other convicts. One of these he singled out. To the mild-mannered, venerable-looking but just as homicidal Miles Thane, he drawled a reminder.

"The south wall. Don't be too close

to it ten minutes from now, but not too far away either. Be ready to make your run when you hear the blast."

"You that sure your plan will work?" challenged Thane, stroking his grey-flecked whiskers.

"It'll work," Alton calmly assured him. "I don't make deals with green-horns, Thane. A sizeable gap will be blasted in that stockade — by an expert. Oh, sure. A real specialist."

"The whole bunch will rush the gap," Thane predicted. "We'll get through, but we'll be running targets." Furtively, he scanned the catwalks atop the high stockade fences bordering the austere sandstone structures of the Bormann Territorial Prison. Rifle-toting guards patroled those catwalks. "Sharpshooters — those bastards."

"The Bormann guards aren't the only sharpshooters in range of us this day," said Alton.

"A lot of flat ground beyond these walls," muttered Thane. "We'll be wide open when we get outside. Some high ground to the south as I recall, but too far to run."

"East for the brush is the only way," said Alton. "The brush is closer and, about fifty yards further east, you'll be in thick timber. Now here's how I figure it. By the time you make the timber, mounted guards will be right behind you. That's your best chance of arming yourselves and getting transportation."

"You mean . . . ?"

"I mean that stand of trees is a fine place for an ambush. Pass the word to other interested parties, Thane. Others of our kind. You know who I mean."

"Billy Bob? Jake and Vern?"

"I think they'll appreciate the suggestion," smiled Alton.

"That makes five of us with something in common," frowned Thane. "Just two choices we have. Make a break for it and take our chances — or spend the rest of our lives in Bormann."

Alton glanced to the clock tower above the administration block.

"Not much longer to wait," he observed.

"How'd you set it up?" demanded Thane. "How'd you make contact with your friends on the outside?"

"Not forgetting Quint Slater, are you?" asked Alton. "I could rely on him. He owed me a favor."

"Discharged last month," recalled Thane.

"Inside twenty-four hours of reaching Bormann City, he delivered a note to an old acquaintance of mine," said Alton. "They've had time enough to follow my instructions — so everything's set." He glanced to the clock-tower again. "Couple more minutes and Johnson and Carew will start a fight. So those catwalk guards will be distracted. Just be ready to make your move, Thane. We're all set."

On the far side of the rise 150 yards south of the big prison, four saddle horses were ground-reined. Atop the rise, three men, well-dressed and well-equipped, made ready to put the

4

Alton plan in motion. Two of them, the burly, grizzle-thatched Carl Craig and the tubby, pig-eyed Gus Pinchon, caressed high-powered rifles fitted with telescopic sights. A third rifle lay beside them ready for the use of the lean and swarthy half-breed now handling a weapon popular with his redskin forebears. Pinchon was the explosives expert of this treacherous trio, Wolf Martell the specialist with bow and arrow. The lank black hair framing his hawk-like visage hung to his shoulders, but no feather jutted from the band of his hat. Like Craig and Pinchon, Martell wore town clothes under his duster.

Gesturing to the bundle lashed to the arrow, Pinchon grinned complacently and assured Craig,

"That bundle packs enough kick to blast the stockade."

"And the fuse — just the right length?" demanded Craig.

"I've calculated it right," bragged Pinchon. "Fuse won't burn down before Wolf puts his arrow in the fence. Way I figure it, she'll detonate when she hits, or maybe a couple seconds after." He fished out a match. "Check the time, Carl."

Craig squinted at his watch. Martell grinned confidently and, as he fitted arrow to bow and tested the string, predicted,

"We'll be seein' your buddy soon, Carl. Betcha life."

"You allowed for the weight of the dynamite?" frowned Craig.

"We practised — remember?" growled Pinchon.

Through a telescopic sight, Craig checked on the movements of the guards, their heads and shoulders visible above the stockade. None were staring this way. The attention of every guard was concentrated on the compound. Right on schedule, two of Alton's fellow-prisoners had obeyed his signal and begun trading blows. Other prisoners were surrounding the brawlers and yelling encouragement

6

while, from the catwalks, the guards bellowed reprimands.

Craig snapped his fingers.

"Okay. Do it!"

Martell rose to a half-kneeling position with the string of the bow drawn back. He fixed his eyes on a section of the stockade and grunted at Pinchon, who scratched the match to life and touched the flame to the end of the dangling fuse. Then Martell loosed the missile, discarded his bow, flopped beside his companions and took up the third rifle. They followed the flight of the arrow with the bundled sticks lashed to its shaft and the fuse spluttering, saw it soar and descend and hit its target, embedding in the fence about 12 inches above ground.

Almost immediately, the charge exploded, blasting an aperture, wreaking havoc. Two guards were toppled from the catwalk to crash into the compound and be set upon by the scum of Bormann, their weapons seized. The din of the blast was still echoing when a half-dozen convicts struggled through the gap and began running for the brush to the east. Alton was among the next half-dozen. He sprinted toward the rise to the south and, at once, Craig, Pinchon and Martell gave him cover.

Three guards sighted the lone runner and swung their rifles to take sight on him, but weren't given time to fire. The men on the rise opened up and the guards were driven off the catwalk by the impact of the well-aimed bullets, two of them dead before crashing into the exercise yard, the third wounded. Moments later, when another dozen yelling prisoners charged through the gap, three hefted the rifles.

"Keep it up!" ordered Craig. "Any guard aiming a rifle this way — make damn sure of him!"

When he reached the north base of the rise, Alton was breathless, but as cold-nerved as ever. He labored up to the summit, darted a glance backward and gasped.

"All right — you did just fine. Now we go."

Craig and the other men followed him down the slant to the south side, sheathed their rifles and raised boots to stirrups. Alton, first to mount, heeled his animal to a hard gallop, setting a breakneck pace. South they rode at speed to reach their first destination some 15 minutes later. They reined up beside a telegraph post in an isolated section. While Craig dismounted and dashed to a hollow log, Pinchon and Martell swung down, hurried into a brush-clump for axes planted there during their journey to the rise; they had thought of everything. Craig tugged a bundle from the hollow log and tossed it to Alton.

"Tie that to your saddle, Cole. No time for you to change here, but we'll be picking up fresh horses at Coon Bend — better place for making the switch."

"Tell those other two to hustle," ordered Alton, as he secured the bulging sack to his saddle.

"They don't need telling," shrugged Craig.

The pole was brought down a few minutes later and the wires and attachments severed and smashed, a delaying tactic Alton's hirelings could not afford to engage in during the run north; a failure in the telegraph service might have been a dead giveaway, alerting the Bormann operator.

This strategy did not prevent the prison's telegrapher from alerting surrounding territories to the breakout. A great many law enforcement agencies were assigning posses to hunt the runaways a full five minutes before Pinchon and Martell damaged the circuit.

But, though they moved quickly, the hunting parties were to be hard at it for the remainder of that day. Seventy inmates of Bormann had made it through the gap before the break was manned by guards.

Other guards pursued the runaways

through the brush and into the timber east of the big pen. Some ran down and recaptured fugitives at gunpoint, shackling them, returning them to the big pen. Others were set upon by desperate felons craving weapons and horses. The ambushers dropped from low-hanging branches or charged out from behind tree-trunks to haul the hapless guards from their mounts and batter them senseless. The pursuit by the prison guards was fast becoming a debacle. Better organized, the hunting parties from Bormann City to the east, Sunday Gulch to the north, Taitville to the south and Hayden to the west were more than a match for the raggletail escapees; the rounding up of runaways was proceeding.

By 8 o'clock that night, bulky Henry Thomson, warden of the Bormann penitentiary, was one mighty harassed and dejected official. He hadn't eaten since 7 a.m. of that day. He was haggard and tired-eyed, slumped behind the desk in his private office and conferring with a trusted confidant, Chief Guard Ira Gaines.

Like his superior, the brawny, heavy-featured Gaines was working on a much-needed shot of whiskey.

"It could've been worse, Mister Thomson," he muttered. "You won't agree — not the way you're feeling — but it *could've* been worse. Forty recaptured and more being brought in."

"I'm thinking of resigning," Thomson said bitterly.

"That'd be a mistake," opined Gaines.

"Thanks for your loyalty, Ira," said Thomson. "I know you mean well, but you should remember my responsibility is greater than yours. You're in charge of the guards. I'm in charge of the whole security program here at Bormann. I plan the system. I give the orders. And today's tragedy will go against my record. The prison board could decide to replace me, even if I don't offer my resignation."

"Tell me how anybody could guess

it'd happen like it did," growled Gaines. "Damn it, you're only human."

"There is no way inmates could improvise an explosive," frowned Thomson. "We don't keep dynamite or blasting powder at Bormann and it's impossible for them to steal cartridges from the armory."

"Armory's under tight guard twenty-four hours a day," said Gaines.

"Plain enough the charge was planted outside the stockade," nodded Thomson. "Whoever planned this breakout had outside help. But how in blazes was it done? We've had bright moonlight this whole month. Our guards watch the surrounding terrain, yet somebody managed to cross the flats and plant that charge. How did they do it, and how was the charge detonated?"

"I'd reckon a bullet," said Gaines.

"So, as well as planting dynamite, they had to mark it so they'd have a target," Thomson pointed out. "And they managed that — undetected by the guards?"

"That's what we have to believe," sighed Gaines. "But don't ask me why they weren't spotted. I'll vouch for every man under my command, Mister Thomson." He emptied his glass, rose and trudged to the window. "There's the bell signaling they're opening the gate again — more runaways being brought in."

"Get down there," urged Thomson, as he poured himself a refill. "There'll be no sleep for me till I know the final tally."

Later, when Gaines rejoined his chief, he called names from a hastily scribbled list. Thomson checked these against a previously compiled list of the escapees.

"If I was a farming man, I'd call that a fair harvest," Gaines said encouragingly. "Seventy made the break. Forty-five rounded up and back in their cells. Eleven dead. Nine wounded, laid up in the infirmary. Only five still on the run."

"With a good chance of evading

the search parties," fretted Thomson. "No moon tonight, Ira. Under cover of darkness, they could travel quite a distance from Bormann County. Let's not forget there are four horses not accounted for." His voice shook as he reminded the chief guard, "*Our* casualties were heavy. Three guards dead, seven seriously injured."

"I hate to admit to myself — one of those five missing men is likely the one who set it all up," muttered Gaines. "I mean, if he was smart enough to plan the break . . . "

"He could be smart enough to cover his tracks and escape the posses," nodded Thomson. "Well now . . . " He consulted his list again, the list on which he had scored out all but five names. "Four of the five we know to be of superior intelligence. Any one of them could be the brain behind the breakout."

"Who's the fifth man?" demanded Gaines.

"William Robertson Grebb — better

known as Billy Bob," said Thomson. "Horse-thief and killer with a wayward streak. Surgeon McDonald, as learned a medical man as I've ever known, described Grebb as a misfit and a dangerous psychopath. Less than a brilliant intellect, Ira, but cunning even so. And deadly." He shook his head in disgust. "Why were any of these five spared the hangrope? Convicted killers, all of them."

"I guess some judges believe a life sentence isn't as merciful as hanging," shrugged Gaines. "And maybe these men didn't rate mercy."

Thomson read out the other names. "Vernon Melville, Jacob Falstead, Miles Thane, Cole Alton."

"The worst!" breathed Gaines. "Damn it, Mister Thomson, of all the scum in Bormann . . . !"

"Yes," Thomson said grimly. "They all drew life sentences, so they've nothing to gain by surrendering to any posse — nothing to lose by killing again. Their kind has no respect for human life, Ira. Maybe not even their own."

"You'll get descriptions circulating fast," guessed Gaines. "Pictures — descriptions — everything."

"I'll do that of course," said Thomson. "And then all we can hope is that they'll run into a trap and be apprehended — before they kill again."

"They're hard to understand," complained Gaines. "Think of the chances they take. Three of those ambushed guards were stripped. The runaways who jumped 'em risked recapture, took time to strip 'em. And you know what *that* means. As well as being mounted and armed, they're wearing civilian clothes."

"I have pleaded with the board to provide uniforms for our guards," said Thomson. "Maybe this will finally convince them."

"Everything too late," scowled Gaines. "That damn board, all those pea-brained big shots."

"For the sake of all the decent

folk of the territory, Grebb and those other runaways have to be recaptured quickly," declared Thomson. "If any of them reaches a big town or a small settlement, any kind of community . . . " His face clouded over, "I pity that place."

★ ★ ★

The place was Alvison, a thriving cattle town and the seat of Alvison County, one of the Wyoming Territory's well-established communities. Two drifters of nomadic but gregarious instincts wandered into it a couple of days later, trail-weary, short on provision, but currently solvent and craving a little town-living — preferably unmarred by violent incident.

Their names were Lawrence Valentine and Woodville Eustace Emerson. They were better known to the press and to a great many lawmen as well as Larry and Stretch; also the press had tagged them the Texas Trouble-Shooters, much to

18

their chagrin. Given a choice, these wanderers would never have raised a fist nor emptied a holster against their fellow-men. Peace-loving they were. Yes, this was their constant claim, but voiced wistfully and with a hint of desperation. Trouble, they had learned to their chagrin, was bent on finding them wherever they roamed. They didn't have to seek out conflicts, life-or-death emergencies, nerve-wracking crises. Such things just happened anyway.

It was sundown when they idled their mounts into Alvison's lively main street and surveyed the buildings lining it, the stores and saloons, the hotels, banks and other such edifices.

"Busy place, this Alvison," the taller Texan observed. "Speakin' for myself now, I'd as soon rest my butt in a busy town than any other kind. Gives me a good feelin', you know? Me floppin', takin' it easy while every other hombre's hustlin' at his chores. We don't have to hustle, huh runt?

Don't need to earn no dinero? How much we got right now?"

"Four hundred and fifty bucks," shrugged Larry Valentine. "Not countin' the thirty dollars stashed in my boot."

"I got twenty hid in my boot," drawled Stretch. "So who needs to work? Not us, ol' buddy. Not us."

How do two compulsive drifters attain such solvency? As well as Larry's poker-savvy and Stretch's occasional lucky streaks at dice or roulette, they did perform well-paid services for deserving folk upon occasion. At all times versatile, they could turn their calloused hands to all manner of chores. Their origin was the Texas Panhandle, so they worked cattle as effortlessly as they breathed in and breathed out. They were horse-breakers when needs be. They had toiled as track-layers for railroads, had ridden escort for freight outfits; name any chore and they could adapt to it.

But outlaw-fighting seemed to have become their main occupation. Try as they might, they could not dodge their hex. And nowadays they were resigned to the fate, half-expecting to lock horns with the lawless — their natural enemies — wherever they showed their weatherbeaten faces. Knights-errant of the 19th Century, the press had called them. The fourth estate had exaggerated their exploits out of all proportion, while the Federal authorities, the U.S. Army, the Pinkerton Detective Agency and some hundreds of town and county peace officers rankled at this purloining of their thunder and strove to minimize their contributions to the peace of the frontier. Rather than accord them celebrity status, such authorities deemed it wiser to dismiss their achievements as freak luck, a consequence of their happening to intrude on the scene of murder or robbery at a crucial moment.

Larry, scanning the buildings to his right, sighted a painted sign and remarked,

21

"Guyatt Hotel looks okay."

Dark-haired and of uncommonly muscular physique, he was the more intuitive half of the much-traveled duo, a ruggedly handsome nomad who stood 6 feet 3 inches bootless, packed a Colt at his right hip and a Winchester in his saddle-scabbard and was fast becoming a cynic, but without danger to his sense of humor or his altruistic attitudes. He straddled a clean-limbed sorrel and, like his partner, favored the garb of the veteran range rider and toted his worldly possession in packroll and saddlebags.

Topping Larry by a full three inches, Stretch had easily earned his nickname. He was a gangling beanpole of a man, tow-haired and homely with his lantern jaw and jughandle ears, easy-going and guileless except when backing his partner in fistic conflict or a shootout. Though he wore twice as much Colt as Larry, that extra .45 at his left hip was no showpiece; he was ambidexterous with handguns. His mount was a pinto.

"Livery stable just a little farther along," he pointed out. "So what d'you say? We bed our critters, rent us a room, down a couple of steaks and then find us a friendly barkeep?"

"And stay out of trouble," Larry said hopefully.

"That's what we always do," insisted Stretch.

"That's what we always *try* to do," countered Larry.

They left their horses in care of a stablehand and toted their packrolls and saddlebags along to the Guyatt Hotel. The desk-clerk, one Al Stroud, presented the register and an inked pen. They scribbled their signatures, were told the going rates and settled for a three-day stay, payment in advance. Narrow-eyed Al Stroud offered the key to a double upstairs and did not appear to notice the thickness of the wallet from which Larry extracted a $50 bill, Larry being the banker of this 20 years or more partnership.

As the clerk made change from the fifty, Larry enquired the location of the nearest restaurant.

"That'd be the Beaver Hat, just around the corner in Rimmer Street," Stroud told him. "Our dining room opens in a half-hour, but maybe you can't wait that long?"

"Not a whole half-hour," grinned Larry, as he gathered up his gear. "That ain't no mountain cat you hear growlin'. It's my partner's belly."

After the new arrivals toted their gear upstairs, Stroud summoned the porter.

"Take over for a few minutes, Sid. I'll be right back."

To Alvison's biggest saloon Stroud hurried. Rober's Palace of Joy had everything the pleasure-bent payday ranch-hand could crave, music, girls, opulent appointments, every popular game of chance and a fine variety of booze dispensed by two hefty bartenders, plus an even heftier bouncer famed for his ability to expel troublesome

24

drunks and sore losers. Big Anse McWhirter's victims did not regard him as the Palace's major attraction, of course. He was standard and necessary equipment, a muscle-bound giant who performed his chores with relish.

It was Big Anse who answered Stroud's question, directing him to a table adjacent to the roulette layout. Stroud approached that table, gave Neeley Rober a high sign and sidled to the stairs to climb half-way to the gallery. The pudgy and dapper half-owner of the saloon joined him there soon afterward.

Behind the joviality of Rober's blotchy, double-chinned visage lurked the mentality of the predatory gyp-artist.

"Just in case they show up here, Mister Rober," mumbled Stroud. "Couple Texans. So tall you couldn't miss 'em. And the dark-haired one — he packs a fat wallet."

"When the pigeons fly into town, I can always rely on good friends to pass me the word," grinned Rober. Under the pretext of shaking Stroud's hand, he squeezed a crumpled bank note into his eager palm. "Much obliged, Al. If Fat-Wallet decides to favor us with his patronage, I'll be ready for him."

From the Beaver Hat cafe, some 70 minutes later, the well-fed drifters sauntered to Main Street. They were at once drawn to the Palace of Joy by the lively music provided by that establishment's four-piece orchestra and, within moments of entering the crowded barroom, were greeted by the proprietor and a runty local devoid of the proprietor's larcenous instincts. Phineas Corkhill, just a shade over 5 feet tall and the elder of Alvison's resident physicians, was impressed by Larry's generous height, but even more so by his partner's. While he squinted up at Stretch and offered his invitation, Larry cocked an ear and eyed Rober enquiringly.

"Didn't catch what you asked," he said. "Kind of noisy in here."

"Asking if poker's your pleasure,"

grinned Rober. "About to start a little five card stud with some good friends of mine, and new blood's always welcome."

"Well, if you got an empty chair, that's as good a place for my butt as any other," Larry said genially. "Big feller . . . ?"

"You go ahead, runt," urged Stretch. "This here's Doc Corkhill and he hankers to buy me a drink, says he wants to ask me a thing or two." He bent almost double to enquire of the little medico, "You drummin' up trade, Doc? Shucks, I ain't feelin' poorly."

"My interest is mostly academic," explained Doc Corkhill.

"I dunno what that means," grinned Stretch. "So I'd best find out, huh?"

And so the Texans separated, Larry accompanying Rober to a poker table, Stretch following Doc to the bar. There, the undersized healer paid for a bottle, took up a couple of glasses and suggested,

27

"We ought to get the load off our feet."

"Fine by me," nodded Stretch. "I just spotted a table nobody's usin'. Let's grab it, 'fore some other hombres get the same idea."

They made it to the unoccupied table and, while Stretch built a cigarette, his diminutive new friend, uncorked the bottle and played barkeep. While thus involved, he talked of the mystery with which he had toyed since graduating from medical school long years before. Ruddy-complexioned and bright-eyed, his goatee matching the snowy hair visible under his back-tilted derby, he spoke earnestly.

"Why do some men grow no taller than my little old self and why do others attain your lofty height? Fascinating question, son. I've grappled with it for years and, when I finally retire from practice, intend writing a paper on the subject."

Stretch was content to relax, throw occasional glances toward his partner and the other poker-players and let Doc Corkhill do most of the talking. Never very demanding of his fellow-men, he was warming to the gabby healer and trying to show polite interest.

Nowadays, he learned, Doc didn't mind leaving most of Alvison's sick to the ministrations of a younger and more energetic colleague. Dr David Howland was only two years out of medical school, quite brilliant in all fields and becoming popular, building a thriving practice. That was fine by Doc, who figured he had earned his rest and a chance to concentrate on his pet preoccupation.

"Has to be a reason, Stretch," he insisted. "Stretch — what an apt nickname for a man who must be all of six feet five."

"Six feet six," offered Stretch. "Without my boots."

"Incredible," enthused Doc. "Most remarkable specimen I've yet encountered — my first six and a half footer! And why, I wonder? Genetics maybe?

Diet? Let's start with the hereditary factor. Were both your parents tall people? Or only your father?"

"My pa was kind of high off the ground," Stretch recalled, glancing to the gambling sector. "About as high as my ol' buddy Larry, meanin' six feet three. Ma, she wasn't as tall as Pa."

"I should hope," frowned Doc.

"Only five feet ten or thereabouts," said Stretch.

"Hell's bells!" gasped Doc.

For better than an hour, the Texans seemed set for a sociable evening. Stretch and the runty medico were talking along like old friends from way back. Larry was winning a pot or two, also losing. By 9 o'clock, he was down $300 and becoming curious, if not actually suspicious.

He had sized up the other players accurately — he hoped. Neeley Rober looked to be typical of a hundred and one gamblers-cum-saloonkeepers he had known over the years, bluff and jovial, always ready with the broad, genial grin. The man at his right had been introduced as Noah Quill, proprietor of a local doss-house. He was scruffy and taciturn and seemed harmless enough. At his left sat the impassive, well-groomed Ed Brinley, sallow-complexioned and saturnine, obviously a professional gambler, a veteran. Undertaker Lloyd Carbro filled the chair closest to Rober. He wore the sombre garb favored by his profession and was as pudgy as Rober, but not as jovial.

Never a sore loser, Larry had played the game many years. He had the skill, the savvy, the instincts of an old riverboat gambler. His gains had been light, his losses heavy. This could be coincidence, the luck of the draw. On the other hand . . .

Rober was dealing when Larry noted what he should have noted earlier in the game, *would* have noted, but for his natural tendency to accord new acquaintances the benefit of the doubt.

"That couldn't be the first time, Rober," he said sharply.

The other men traded glances. Feigning puzzlement, Rober asked, "First time for what? I don't know what you mean."

"You slipped yourself a card from under the deck," said Larry. "That was plenty slick. You're good at it. But I ain't applaudin'."

"You have the nerve to accuse me of . . . ?" began Rober.

"I don't mind droppin' three hundred in an honest gamble," declared Larry. "But not his way."

"Careful how you talk, Valentine," warned Brinley. "Neeley Rober always deals square."

"Always," Quill said quickly. "Mister Rober's no cheat."

"I'll vouch for Neeley any time," asserted Carbro.

Rober had discarded the deck in a fine show of exasperation. Now, with both hands under the table, he began a reprimand.

"If you can't take your losses like a gentleman, if you have to cry cheat when you lose a few hundred in an honest game . . . "

"Hogwash," scowled Larry. "You're a sharper and, the way it sounds, these other hombres are in cahoots with you."

"Keep your hands on the table, Valentine," grinned Rober. "I've got a derringer aimed at your belly."

2

Epilogue to a Set-up

"I'M starting to bore you, huh?" Doc Corkhill sadly challenged. "You aren't listening. Well, I guess I can't blame you . . . "

"'Scuse me, Doc," frowned Stretch. Though the barroom crowd was milling, he had a clear view of the poker table. "I don't mean to be impolite. It's just I don't like the way my partner looks."

Doc rose, the better to study the scene.

"I see what you mean," he said. "And I wouldn't care to be the man your partner's looking at. Not the way he's looking."

"I'd best get on over there," Stretch said apologetically, as he vacated his chair.

At any other time, a derringer under

34

a table might have deterred Larry. But now Rober was adding insult to injury, ordering him to leave.

"Get out of my saloon — cheapskate. And be thankful I'm not sending for the sheriff."

That did it for Larry. He had been sitting with his legs crossed. The hell with the risks. His right leg parted company with his left and swung sideways. Simultaneously, he scooped up a glasss and hurled the contents into Rober's face. He felt his boot make hard contact with Rober's hand, heard the sneak-gun clatter to the floor. From his left, Brinley promptly swung at him. The tinhorn's fist struck his ear and, growling ferociously, he retaliated with his left elbow. The jab won a grunt of anguish from Brinley.

"Pete! Horrie . . . !" bellowed Rober, recoiling from the table, dabbing at his eyes.

At that, the barkeeps vaulted the bar and advanced on Larry, who rose up quickly, overturning the table.

"That better be an end to it, fellers!" advised the approaching Stretch.

But it was obvious Rober's staff had been hired for their fistic ability as much as their talent for serving booze or supervising games of chance. While the barkeeps rushed Larry, the faro, dice and roulette dealers converged threateningly at Stretch.

Non-combatants began a rush to safe vantagepoints or to get the hell out of here, depending on their inclinations, some fearing they might become involved, some relishing a pitched brawl and craving to watch the action. Doc Corkhill just happened to have another preoccupation; as well as his favorite enigma — why so short and why so tall — he enjoyed a good fight. With surprising agility, he quickly attained the best possible viewing position for a man his size by scrambling atop a corner table. From there, he watched the barkeeps attack Larry and come to grief.

A hard blow from his first assailant

didn't shake Larry, only served to fire his fury. He struck back with a punch so powerful that his attacker lost consciousness before hitting the floor. The second barkeep telegraphed his first blow and wasn't given time for another. Larry ducked that swing, slammed his left to the belly and loosed a right uppercut, sending his bloody-mouthed victim reeling three yards to crash against the cursing Neeley Rober. To Larry's chagrin, Brinley, Quill and Carbro were giving him a wide berth. He hungered to give them the feel of his fists, but now had another threat to face. Eyes a'gleam, big fists raised, the massive bouncer was advancing on him.

Stretch's three attackers, meanwhile, were sincerely regretting having attacked him. The roulette man lost interest after landing a punch and suffering punishment. Stretch's rock-hard left exploded in his face like a mule's kick and drove him all the way to the bar, but not to order a drink; he struck the front of the bar, collapsed and slept. The faro and dice supervisors were keeping up the attack, closing with the taller Texan, grappling fiercely. It was their earnest desire to force him off his feet and pin him to the floor, but they were doomed to disappointment. While the onlookers guffawed and yelled encouragement, while the percentage-girls giggled and shrieked from the safety of the gallery, Stretch maneuvered to get handholds on the collars of two well-tailored coats, then proceeded to bat two heads together — hard. The impact caused many to wince and was not appreciated by the faro and dice man, both of whom crumbled untidily.

The first of Larry's assailants revived and, snarling obscenities, smashed a bottle against the bar-edge. Gripping the neck and the jagged section adhering, he charged at Stretch, forcing him to dodge and duck his murderous swinging and jabbing.

Big Anse McWhirter was vainly

attempting to get the better of a wily adversary, his big fists threshing and missing. Relying on fast footwork to avoid those wild blows or, worse, a bear-hug that would have cracked his ribs, Larry was biding his time, watching for openings. His bunched left swung fast, plunging into the vulnerable area just above the big man's belt-buckle. The bouncer made a growling, wheezing sound and grasped at him. He backstepped, braced himself and unwound an uppercut, the swing starting from far below the bottom of his holster, soaring up at rocket-like speed to make harsh contact with the unprotected jaw. McWhirter lurched backward, shuddering. An uproar of cheers rose deafeningly as Larry lunged at the giant to land three more blows, two to the midriff and another mighty uppercut; the whole saloon seemed to vibrate to the echoing thud as McWhirter hit the floor.

Larry wasn't ready for what happened next. No new challengers confronted him but, from his rear, a six-gun roared, the din of the report startling the crowd to silence. The lick of the bullet three inches under his right armpit filled him with fiery pain, shocked him and buffeted him off-balance. Whirling, fearing the wound would impede his emptying his holster, he glowered at the shooter.

The man was lean, many a year his junior, flashily garbed and coolly recocking a gleaming, nickel-plated Colt. Larry had a blurred impression of a snow-white Stetson crowning a leering face, a black jacket and grey-striped pants, in the instant that he got his left hand to a chairback, whisked the chair from the floor and hurled it all in one swift movement. The chair struck the dapper gunman's mid-section, causing him to lose his grip of the pistol. As that weapon thudded to the floor, Larry charged at him in blind rage, seized him, lifted him off his feet and flung him at the street-window. To the accompaniment of a crash of breaking glass, the window was demolished and the human missile consigned to the sidewalk.

During the uproar following that exhibition of brute strength, Larry retrieved his hat and sidled to where his partner was blowing on his knuckles and genially acknowledging the applause of an over-stimulated audience.

"Sonofabitch — tried to backshoot me . . . !"

"Let me take a look, runt." Stretch bent to squint. Well now, it don't bleed much. I'd reckon he only nicked your hide."

"While my back was turned!" fumed Larry.

"Don't seem like it slowed your right arm any," Stretch offered as consolation. "I saw you use both hands to hurl that dud through the window."

"If that bastard ever tries me face to face . . . " began Larry.

He left that sentence unfinished. The Alvison County law was now arriving.

The sheriff, bulky, florid and triple-chinned, was glowering at the Texans, brandishing a .45 and cocking an ear to the demands voiced by Neeley Rober. These strangers, Rober asserted, had started a disturbance on his premises and had beaten up a half-dozen of his staff. Worse than that, one of them had assaulted Deputy Prince. Who, wondered Stretch, was Deputy Prince?

The answer to that question caused Larry to grimace in disgust. The dapper man now re-entered to retrieve his shining, pearl-butted Colt. Cursing bitterly, bleeding from several cuts, he peeled off his black coat to shake it, to rid it of slivers of glass. Only then did Larry sight the star gleaming on his fancy vest.

"By glory!" boomed the sheriff. "No trail-trash gonna get away with *that*! Assaultin' a law officer in my bailiwick? You saddlebums're jailbait!" He aimed his Colt at the tall men. "Deputy Milhauser, I'm arrestin' these strangers.

You move round behind 'em and take their sidearms." He added, scathingly, "Let's see if you can do *that* right."

"I'll be swearing other charges, Sheriff," announced Rober. "Those drifters attacked employees of this establishment and . . . "

"You lyin' sonofabitch!" scowled Larry.

"I've got witnesses!" declared Rober.

"It's just like Mister Rober says, Sheriff," offered Quill.

"Absolutely," nodded Brinley.

To that, undertaker Carbro added, "We saw the whole thing. They started it, nothin' surer."

"Milhauser!" thundered the sheriff. "What the hell're you waitin' for?"

Despite their anger, the Texans switched their attention to the burly, solemn-faced lawman advancing on them. The second deputy was blunt-featured, the blond hair at his temples showing grey flecks, his garb strictly utilitarian, contrasting sharply with the showy attire of the malicious Prince.

He was hefting a shotgun, but hadn't cocked it.

"Best come along," he said quietly, as he drew closer.

Larry had abandoned hope of intervention by other witnesses. Plainly, Rober exerted a heavy influence on the townmen patronizing the Palace of Joy. Either that, or they hadn't observed the first blows were swung by Rober's hirelings. With his wound smarting, but his ire cooling, he decided against offering resistance. He slipped his holster-thong, unstrapped his gunbelt and held it out to the burly deputy with the sad eyes. Stretch followed his example.

"Two-gun man," jeered the sheriff, as the deputy took the proffered weapons. "Got us a real hotshot pistolero here. Come on, Jesse, and you, Milhauser. Let's get 'em to where they belong."

Why hadn't little Doc Corkhill protested the lies voiced by Rober and his hangers-on? Stretch wondered about that while moving out with Larry, prodded by the guns of Jesse Prince and his big-bellied boss. They were trudging the sidewalk with Deputy Milhauser leading, when Doc reappeared, toting his valise.

"Doggone it, Doc, you saw the whole thing . . . " Stretch began.

"Got something more important on my mind right now," muttered Doc. "Your friend's wound needs attention. Don't worry about anything else, my way-up-there friend. I'll say my piece where it'll count most."

"Tomorrow — what d'you say?" Prince was urging the sheriff.

"Why the hell not?" grinned the boss-lawman. "Court'll be in session anyway, so we might's well get these Johnny-come-latelies tried and sentenced and off our hands. I don't relish stinkin' up my jail with Texas riff-raff."

"Hear that, big man?" Prince taunted Larry. "You get yours two o'clock tomorrow at the county courthouse."

"You know somethin', runt?" frowned Stretch. "Just this once, we ought to

45

hire us a lawyer. We got cash enough, or did that Rober hombre take you for our whole roll?"

"No talkin'!" ordered the sheriff. "Jesse, when we got these no-accounts locked up, I want you to hustle back to the palace and get all the depositions on paper. Find the justice of the peace, get sighed and witnessed affidavits, ask Lawyer Gregory if he wants to defend 'em. Or that new lawyer? I can't never remember his name. You know? The dumb kid?"

Fifteen minutes later, having been installed in a double cell of the county jail by Sheriff Cleaver Moss and Deputy Milhauser, their sidearms hung on the gunrack, Larry's wallet containing some $150 locked in the office safe, the Texans waxed curious that their case would be so soon heard. With them was the busy Doc Corkhill. And as gabby as ever. He answered their question while checking on Larry's wound.

"It'll be tomorrow, because you don't have to wait for a circuit-judge. Orin

Blake used to ride circuit, but that was before his illness slowed him down. He settled here in Alvison, lives with his daughter on Mailey Street. So now he's our resident judge."

"Our case gets heard by a sick judge?" grouched Stretch.

"Nothing wrong with Judge Blake's brain," Doc assured him. "He's crippled with arthritis and, believe me, that's no mental disorder. My young colleague Davy Holland does what he can — which is more than *I* could do." He shrugged impatiently. "Arthritis. Maybe a new name for an old ailment. I wouldn't know. Damn it, young Davy is way ahead of me in many fields."

"You good with gunshot wounds?" Larry asked with a bleak grin.

"Good enough, Larry," nodded Doc. "Your middle name should be 'Lucky'. You have an ugly bullet-burn, but the slug barely tore your skin. How does that dressing feel? Less pain now?"

"Feels just fine," said Larry, as he began redonning the top half of his underwear. "How much do I owe you?"

"No charge for any friend of Stretch," Doc said amiably.

"Now, Doc," growled Larry, tugging off a boot. "You got to understand I appreciate the kindly thought, but I don't aim to owe no man in this town. Not after what happened at Rober's place — all the cheatin' and lyin'. So name your fee."

"If you insist, a dollar is plenty," shrugged Doc.

"Keep your boot on, runt," drawled Stretch. "I got it."

Doc pocketed a silver dollar, closed his bag and called from the cell-door, "I'm finished. Come let me out."

"Hold on now, Doc," frowned Stretch. "You ain't said how much of that ruckus you saw."

"You could be our only witness," Larry pointed out.

"Relax," soothed the little man. "Don't deprive me of a chance to make a grandstand play in court. At the right moment, I'll come forward on your behalf. Meanwhile, it'll be interesting to see just how far Rober and his pals will go."

Some 20 minutes after releasing Doc from the cell and ushering him out, the burly deputy re-entered the jailhouse toting four tin cups on a tray. The Texans were then reminded they weren't the only inmates of this calaboose. From cells further along the passage, prisoners Rudolph Lucas and Thadeus 'Jug' Updike greeted the deputy with plaintive cries.

"Have a heart, Dutch, begged Lucas. "That coffee ain't fit for hogs."

"Drink it and be thankful, Rudy," muttered Milhauser.

"Aw, c'mon, Dutch!" whined Updike. "I need a *real* drink! You could organize me a shot of good rye, couldn't you? I wouldn't ask the sheriff or that mean dude Prince, but you bein' a gentleman . . . !"

"Cut it out, Jug," chided Milhauser. "You know it has to be water or jailhouse coffee or nothin'. I don't relish losin' my badge by sneaking booze to you. I need to *keep* this job."

He distributed coffee to Lucas and Updike, the latter enquiring,

"What d'you want with a tin star anyway, Dutch? You're too good-hearted to be a lawman."

Milhauser didn't answer that question. Reaching the door of the double cell, he nodded to the new prisoners.

"Might's well try it," he suggested. "I drink it sometimes. You've likely tasted as bad on a trail drive."

The Texans rose from their bunks and trudged to the bars to accept the brimming cups and warily test the coffee.

"You're right," said Larry. "We've tasted worse. And better."

"Take your time drinkin' it," offered Milhauser. "I have to wait anyway."

"For what?" asked Stretch.

"Dutch has to take these tin cups away." Lucas called an explanation.

"There was this fool tried to kill himself a couple years ago."

"With a tin cup?" blinked Stretch.

"Real strong feller — and a mite tetched," said Lucas. "Tore the handle right off, jabbed the broke end into his throat."

"But they couldn't blame Dutch for *that* " recalled Updike. "He wasn't on duty. Deputy Pretty-Gun Prince was."

Larry sipped coffee and traded appraisals with the deputy.

"First name's Larry, Dutch," he drawled. "The stringbean's called Stretch."

"I know," nodded Milhauser. "Heard of you a time or two. I don't think Sheriff Moss or Jesse Prince ever did, but I have."

"You feel like talkin'?" prodded Larry.

"We're curious about a couple of things," said Stretch.

Anything I can tell you," shrugged Milhauser.

"Your boss and that Rober hombre,

they're good buddies?" demanded Larry.

"Partners," said Milhauser. "Cleaver Moss is half-owner of the Palace."

"Now ain't that cosy?" jibed Stretch. "We should've guessed."

"You'll get a fair enough trial," muttered Milhauser.

"With Rober and his pals lyin' their lousy heads off?" growled Larry. "Some fair trial."

"It'll be fair," Milhauser promised. "On account of Judge Blake is fair."

"Who gets to defend us?" demanded Larry.

"Only three lawyers in Alvison," said Milhauser. "Mister Edmunds is county prosecutor. Mister Gregory ain't interested. Seemed he read the depositions and didn't want any part of the case. So you'll have to settle for the new man, the young feller. Name of Kipp. He's in the office right now. Already talked to the witnesses. When he gets through readin' their statements, he'll come visit you."

Larry drained his cup, but did not

surrender it rightaway; he had another question.

"Somethin' else I'm curious about," he told the deputy. "You can invite me to mind my own blame business or you can explain it. Your choice, Dutch."

"What d'you want to know?" frowned Milhauser.

"Moss talks down to you," said Larry. "Acts like he don't much respect you. He got a reason?"

"Ain't many Alvison people respect me," shrugged Milhauser. "Only reason I'm still wearin' this badge is Roy Dent put in a good word for me with Mayor Grove. That was a year ago when the Settlers Trust Bank was robbed. Sheriff Moss and Banker Ellis, they'd have made me turn in my badge but for Mister Dent talkin' up for me."

"Dent packs more weight then a banker?" prodded Stretch.

"He runs the Alvison newspaper, the Sentinel," said Milhauser. "Got important friends all over the county."

"If you don't want to talk about that

bank robbery . . . " began Larry.

"I don't care any more," said Milhauser. "Maybe, this time, I can make somebody understand — and believe."

He recounted the circumstances of his fall from grace quietly, confining himself to the bare facts.

It could have happened to any lawman, the Texans conceded. So why not bone-headed Cleaver Moss or his cousin, the younger deputy with the fancy gun and the urge to make a name for himself? But no. It had to happened to Emil Milhauser, that quiet morning a year ago.

Milhauser was about to stroll past the Settlers Trust when three seemingly harmless strangers jostled him. A gun was shoved into his belly. He was hustled into the bank, his pistol unloaded and returned to his holster, while manager Luther Ellis and his cashier transferred all the bank's funds from the safe to the sack held by one of the bandits. Another kept a cocked

Colt aimed at Milhauser's head from left of the bank entrance. Milhauser was forced to lounge in the doorway, to smile and trade nods and waves with locals passing by. With one of Alvison's lawmen right there in the bank entrance, who could suspect a robbery was in progress? Ellis and his cashier were knocked senseless, but the hapless Milhauser gagged, his ankles tied, his hands secured behind his back with his own manacles. He was still struggling to rid himself of that gag when the thieves departed by way of the rear exit, mounted the horses awaiting them in the back alley and took off. Ellis then regained consciousness.

"And saw me there," Milhauser said bitterly. "Helpless and useless. I'd worked the gag loose. Tried to talk to him, but he wasn't listenin'. Hell, no. He was runnin' off at the mouth, callin' me all kinds of names, mostly 'fool' and 'coward', and I just couldn't make him understand. Those three smart jaspers were never caught.

Cleaver Moss and Cousin Jesse, they'll just never let me live it down. Only man who understood was Roy Dent. Even wrote about me in the paper, said as how it could've happened to any other lawman — includin' Moss or Prince."

"And that," said Larry, "is exactly how I feel."

"Well, sure," nodded Stretch. "Smartest, toughest, bravest lawman west of the Missouri couldn't buck a cocked iron proddin' his belly."

"The banker don't see it that way," said Milhauser. "And that goes double for Moss and Prince — and near every citizen of Alvison. The only friends I got in this town, I could count on the fingers of one hand."

"But you're stayin' on," guessed Larry.

"Damn right." The deputy nodded grimly. "If I quit, some loose-mouthed know-it-all would claim I'm ashamed to face the people. So I'm stayin', sure. Every day I work at keepin' the peace. I earn what the county pays me. Hasn't been any big trouble since the bank robbery, so I've had no chance to prove I'm as good as Moss or Prince."

"Both of 'em," opined Stretch.——

"But the time'll come," Milhauser predicted. "There'll be some kind of emergency, real trouble, the worst kind. Then we'll see if Big-Mouth Moss can handle it. Then we'll see if his fast-draw Cousin Jesse is as good as he claims."

"Somebody ought to take that shiny Colt away from Jesse," declared Stretch. "It'll be the death of him. Hell, it was near the death of Larry."

"Uh huh," grunted Milhauser. "I heard he took a shot at Valentine."

Through clenched teeth, Larry muttered,

"When my back was turned. Damn that trigger-happy dude." He stared hard at Milhauser. "He's Moss' idea of a good deputy — a smart lawman?"

"For Moss' money, Cousin Jesse is one helluva peace officer — and I'm a loser," said Milhauser. He shrugged self-consciously. "I talk too much. Let me have your cups. Okay for the young feller to come visit now?"

"His name's . . . ?" asked Larry.

"Kipp — Warren Kipp," said Milhauser. "Listen, maybe he's smarter then he looks. I mean, if he graduated from law school, if he's got a regular diploma and a licence to practice, he's just got to be a lawyer, right? No matter if he acts kind of awkward?" He threw in a warning. "And it beats tryin' to fight your own case. Even a judge as fair as Orin Blake mightn't take kindly to that."

"We aint goin' anywhere," said Larry.

"Not till around quarter of two tomorrow," said Milhauser, "when you travel to the courthouse in the jail-wagon."

"No place to go and nothin' else to do," drawled Larry. "So we might's well chew the fat with the lawyer-boy."

Milhauser collected the four cups

and returned to the office. When he returned a few moments later, he was accompanied by the most diffident, the most self-conscious young man either drifter had encountered in a month of Sundays. Warren Kipp was around 5 feet 9, but seemed shorter for his stoop-shouldered stance. His grey town suit was well-brushed as was the derby toted in the crook of his left arm. Under the other arm was a sheaf of papers. This shaggy-haired, bespectacled tyro had fallen on hard times. His shirt-cuffs were frayed; the suit and the derby had seen better days, a great many of them. Any way you looked at humble, self-effacing Warren, there was little to impress, little to inspire confidence.

The tall men were taken aback, dubious, but also sympathetic, unable to suppress their long-standing concern for the lowly and oppressed. Yes, with the Warren Kipps of the frontier, they were always gentle.

As he unlocked the cell-door,

Milhauser told the young lawyer,

"Stay as long as you want, son. Just holler when you're ready to leave."

"That's — that's most obliging and generous of you, Deputy Milhauser." Warren thanked him fervently; it was as though the deputy had conferred a great honor on him. "I have to say — I could wish Sheriff Moss' attitude were — half as reasonable — and as friendly."

From their bunks, the tall Texans watched Milhauser open the cell-door for their visitor, usher him in, then resecure it. He returned to the office. They sat up, swung their feet to the floor and nodded affably.

"Howdy," grunted Stretch.

"Warren Kipp, attorney at law, at your service." Moving toward them to offer his hand, Warren managed to drop derby and documents and trip over the latter. Stretch rose in time to break his fall and, after trading dubious glances with Larry, sat him on his bunk, retrieved the fallen items, placed them in his lap and squatted beside his partner. "Thank you, Mister . . . ?"

"Emerson," frowned Stretch.

"Valentine," frowned Larry. "You okay, boy?"

"I tend to be clumsy at times," Warren said apologetically. "And now, gentlemen, if you wish to retain me as defense counsel . . . "

"I guess you're all we got," said Larry.

"Thank you," said Warren, fumbling with his papers. "I intend, of course, to defend you as — uh — forcefully as I'm able, but I should warn you there is little hope of your being acquitted of the charges sworn by Mister Neeley Rober — and other plaintiffs — including Deputy Prince."

"Deputy Prince took a shot at me," said Larry.

"He asserts you were about to draw your pistol, Mister Valentine," warned Warren. "And that he had no option but to deter you."

"He's a liar," growled Larry.

"I may call you to testify to that effect," frowned Warren. "I say I *may* call you, Mister Valentine. If, in my opinion, there is any danger of your showing a belligerent attitude in court, I'll have to use my discretion. I hope you understand that." He adjusted his spectacles and shrugged nervously. "An outburst, a show of anger, might displease Judge Blake. It is my duty — as your lawyer — to warn you against offending His Honor."

"I'll remember that," Larry promised. "No chance of an acquittal, you say?"

"The weight of evidence," said Warren. "The injuries inflicted on the plaintiffs and, in particular, the — uh — rough treatment accorded Deputy Prince."

"I didn't know he was a deputy," said Larry. "His badge wasn't showin'."

"Are you absolutely certain?" Warren asked hopefully.

"I couldn't see it through his doggone coat," said Larry.

"Good point." Warren made a

note of that. "Now, gentlemen, what other points can be raised on your behalf? Extenuating circumstances? As it's almost certain Judge Blake will find for the plaintiffs, our obvious course is a plea for leniency. I mean, with Mister Casper Edmunds prosecuting, with almost a dozen witnesses testifying against you . . . "

"You talked to Doc Corkhill?" asked Stretch.

"Not yet," said Warren. "I know he has offered to testify on your behalf and I'll certainly confer with him as soon as possible. However, as he'll be our only witness, you must resign yourself to the inevitable. You can, of course, insist on trial by jury."

"We'll take our chances with the judge," Larry decided.

"Very wise, I'm sure," nodded Warren. "And now . . . " he balanced a pad on his knees and took up his pencil again. "Your side of the story, gentlemen, if you please."

"Better you tell it, runt," opined

Stretch. "What can I say? I headed for that poker table on account of you were lookin' plenty fazed. Then three hombres jumped me and I just naturally defended myself."

"Rober invited me to play," said Larry. "Introduced me to his buddies — the tinhorn, Quill and the undertaker." He went on to recount the circumstances leading up to his confrontation with the saloon-owner, then offered a blow by blow account of the ensuing melee, plus his set-to with the bouncer, his wounding by Prince and his reaction to the sting of a bullet fired from behind his back. "You want me to admit I got mad? Son, you better believe it. And, for that, I ain't apologizin'. Not to the judge. Not to anybody."

"Very well," frowned Warren. "But — please remember. If I do call you to the stand to repeat what you've told me, try to speak calmly, keep your anger under tight control."

"You got to admit, runt, young

Warren gives good advice," remarked Stretch.

"I got to admit," nodded Larry.

During this conference in Cell 6 of the Alvison County Jail, one of the vengeance-hungry runaways from the Bormann prison munched roasted jackrabbit by his campfire. Jacob Falstead, hefty, shaggy-browed and wary-eyed, squatted with his back to his fire the better to watch for intruders. He wore clothing stripped from a guard whose head he had stove in with a rifle-butt, plus a jacket acquired from a homestead in an isolated area he had ridden through yesterday. That homestead had also been good for a few canned goods, a jug of home-made whiskey and a better mount than the animal once ridden by a guard.

Now, his late supper finished, this hefty, homicidal rogue fingered a bullet, baring his teeth as he studied it.

"This one's for you, Judge Orin Blake," he said softly. "That old newspaper at the homestead — lucky

I fetched it along. So now I know you ain't ridin' circuit no more. Now I know where to find you. And, when I do — this slug's for right between your eyes."

3

Forebodings

TOWARD midnight, Louise Dent, long-suffering but always patient wife of the Sentinel's founder-editor, roused from slumber by the night chill, rose from bed and felt her way to the window. Having closed it, she cocked an ear to a sound from down below. The living quarters of the Dents occupied the second floor of the old building on the corner of Harper and Main, the ground floor accommodating the newspaper office and, out back, her kitchen. Fearing the worse, she lit the lamp.

"Oh, mercy," she sighed. "Not again."

Upon retiring around 9.45, she had assumed her husband would do likewise soon afterward. But no. His side of the bed was unoccupied, his folded nightshirt still on his pillow. She heaved another sigh as she donned robe and slippers and quit the bedroom. Descended to the newspaper office, her worst fear was confirmed.

As alert, as wide-awake as ever, Roy Dent seemed to have lost track of time. Old files were heaped on his desk, clippings from other Wyoming papers scattered about. He was perched on the high stool at a filing cabinet, rummaging, mumbling to himself, when she called to him sharply.

"Roy, for heaven's sake, it's near midnight. You aren't as young as you used to be and young Doctor Howland has warned you're an ideal candidate for a heart attack. Roy, you need your sleep!"

"Can't sleep yet," he muttered. "Not till I'm through checking. Glad you came down, Lou. I could use . . . "

"All right, all right." She shrugged resignedly and turned toward the rear door leading into the kitchen. "I'll light the stove again, start the coffee brewing."

"Not coffee," he growled. "I could use some help here. Got a couple more names to cross-check."

Balding, bespectacled, slight of physique and prematurely aged, Roy Dent was no placid take-your-time frontier editor. He was erudite, impatient and sometimes too excitable for his own good, his whole demeanor typical of the high-pressure attitudes of big city journalists.

"And what, may I enquire, brought on this fever of file-checking?" she demanded.

"That bulletin on the Bormann breakout," he frowned. "Names of the five escapees still at large. Familiar, Lou. Haven't been able to shake 'em out of my mind since the bulletin arrived. Got this bad feeling rightaway. A premonition of danger. And, by Godfrey, I just know I'm *right*!"

"Very well," she nodded. "Tell me about it."

"There's a connection, I'm sure of

69

that," he declared, rummaging again. "Orin — and those five runaway killers. I've already turned up two names, Melville and Alton. Do me a favor, Lou. Start checking back issues of the Bodeyville Messenger and the Kemp City Gazette."

"How far back?"

"Four — five years."

"And what am I looking for?"

"Court reports. Murder trials heard before Orin."

"Oh, you mean — while he was still a circuit-judge?"

"What the hell else?"

"Don't be irritable," chided Lou, as she went to work.

"Up until Orin's wife died, you were a good friend of hers," he reminded her. "If you'd suspected Nell was in danger of being murdered, *you'd* have been irritable — wouldn't you have?"

"Poor Nell died of pneumonia," said Lou.

"In her bed," Dent said bluntly. "And I'd prefer Orin went the same way. Better that — than for his life to be cut short by a bullet."

"Dear Lord — no!" she gasped.

"Keep checking," he urged.

"What of these men whose names you mentioned?" she asked.

"Melville and Alton," said Dent. "They sure have something in common. Ah!" He held up another cutting. "The Thane trial! And Thane made the same threat!"

"Roy, you're confusing me," she complained. "At least give me an inkling of what this is all about."

"Melville, Alton and Thane, all convicted killers," said Dent. "All tried before Judge Orin Blake in different towns along his circuit, all sentenced to life imprisonment. Orin could rarely bring himself to deliver the death sentence."

"And now — those three have escaped?" she frowned. "Well — is there something else they have in common?"

"After Orin passed sentence, there

were outbursts from these killers," muttered Dent. "They cursed the judge, swore oaths of vengeance."

"You mean . . . ?" she began.

"Yes," he nodded. "Death threats."

Lou Dent was worriedly silent, her husband too, until some ten minutes later. Her hand trembled as she laid a clipping on his desk.

"The trial of one Jacob Falstead," she murmured. "At Bodeyville — four and a half years ago."

He scanned the report and grimaced.

"Same thing. Falstead swore he'd kill Orin after being found guilty and sentenced to life imprisonment. Now the Kemp City cuttings, Lou."

"Can you recall a name?"

"Let me think. Rigg? No. Gregg. That's not it. Wait a minute! Grebb! Check under 'G' in the alphabetical list in case I cross-filed it."

Another ten minutes and Roy Dent's hunch was confirmed. His wife had located a report of the Grebb trial at Kemp City three years before. For the first time since his back-checking began, he acknowledged his near-exhaustion; he slumped in his chair and stifled a yawn.

"That cinches it, Lou," he said wearily. "First thing tomorrow, I'll visit the sheriff's office and pass on my warning. Have to look in on Orin too. Well, Lou? Quite a coincidence, huh? Five of them. All killers. All free. And all remembering the judge who sentenced them."

"I call it a frightening coincidence," she declared. "But surely they'll be recaptured?"

"The question is — how soon?" he countered. "And I think I can guess what Cleaver Moss will say." He scowled at the papers littering his desk. "None of them would dare show up in Alvison. That'll be Moss' reaction. Not the brightest lawman I've ever known, our sheriff. Of course there's no guarantee any of them *will* head this way. Some would claim it's too far-fetched, a wild idea."

"Some," she agreed. "Sheriff Moss for instance?"

"Him for sure," he sighed. "But I still have to warn them. The least I can do, Lou. You know how close we are, Orin and I."

"Because Orin enjoys intelligent discussion, good conversation," she said with a wistful smile. "Because he's a gentleman of refinement with a fine mind and, in all of this territory, there are less than a half-dozen men with whom he can enjoy good talk on his own level — and you're one of them. Since he became a cripple, what other pleasure does he have?"

"Well, I guess Phoebe's one of his consolations," he said, rising, yawning again. "Fine young lady, now that she's of age. Orin couldn't wish for a nicer daughter. A credit to him. And to Nell, may she rest in peace."

He killed the lamp and took his wife's arm. As they climbed the stairs, she pointed out,

"Phoebe won't stay with her father

74

forever. That's too much to expect of her, Roy. She's attractive — and eligible. And I'm told Ross Gregory is courting her."

Dent grinned tiredly.

"The other young lawyer too," he assured her.

"That poor, awkward Kipp boy?" she gasped. "Roy, you're joking!"

"Poor, awkward and homely, but very attentive," said Dent. "I don't imagine the so handsome and urbane Gregory thinks of young Kipp as a rival. It's a fact nevertheless. Kipp has been seen moving gingerly up the walk to the porch of Orin's home, his derby in one hand, a posy in the other. You have to admit that's what lawyers call pretty conclusive evidence. Unless you want to believe the posy was for my friend Orin."

★ ★ ★

The Sentinel editor made an early visit to the sheriff's office next morning, arriving while Moss was assigning his deputies their duties for the day. Squatting on the couch by the north wall, Jesse Prince was studying his reflection in a shaving mirror, scowling at the iodine-painted cuts on his cheeks and brow, his legacy of last night's headlong plunge through the front window of the Palace of Joy. Milhauser was over by the stove, setting the prisoners' breakfasts on a tray.

"You'll be testifyin', Jesse, which means me and you both have to be in court," muttered the sheriff. "Milhauser, after you're through feedin' the prisoners, you'll walk mornin' patrol. Also, come quarter of two, you'll have the team hitched to the rig and be ready to drive the prisoners to the courthouse." He nodded to the newspaperman. "'Mornin', Dent. Listen, I got no time for you right now. Kind of busy."

"It won't take but a few moments, and it's important," said Dent.

"Well, make it quick, huh?" urged Moss.

"About that bulletin from Bormann," said Dent, helping himself to a chair. "I take it you've had no word on the five uncaptured runaways? Nothing from the telegraph office?"

"Nothin' yet," shrugged Moss. "I'm not worryin' about 'em. Got my hands full with tendin' my own bailiwick. There's posses huntin' 'em all over. I figure they'll be rounded up inside twenty-four hours."

"They don't stand a chance," asserted Prince, still absorbed in his mirror.

No chance at all," agreed Moss.

"'Morning, Dutch, and you too, Deputy Prince," nodded Dent.

"Mister Dent." Milhauser showed him a brief grin.

"Well now, about those escapees," said Dent. "I wouldn't be too sure they'll be run to ground so quickly, Sheriff. I've been checking the reports on their trials. Killers, all five of them."

"Includin' Billy Bob Grebb, him

that's supposed to be one helluva gunfighter," sneered Prince. "Hey, I hope I run into that hotshot. I'd back him down fast and, if he dared try drawin' on me — that'd be the end of him."

"Billy Bob's dangerous," frowned Dent. "The other four are worse. County prosecutors at their trials described them as being extremely intelligent." He stared hard at Moss. "Give that some thought, Sheriff. Extremely intelligent. So probably smart enough to dodge the search parties and come right here to Alvison."

"That's crazy," scoffed Moss. "Last place they'd try to hide in is a town like Alvison."

"Maybe not," argued Dent. "The bigger the town, the more hiding places, the more chance of passing unnoticed."

"We got pictures and descriptions," said Prince. "If they came to Alvison, that'd be one real bad mistake. Cleaver or me, we'd spot'em for sure."

"You or the sheriff," nodded Dent. "Or Dutch."

"I wouldn't count on Milhauser recognizin' 'em," jibed Prince. We know how smart *he* is. Proved it, didn't he? When the Settlers Trust was taken for every last dollar?"

"With help from Milhauser," scowled Moss. "What's holdin' you up, Milhauser? Get in there with that chow. I don't want them calaboose trash whinin' we're starvin' 'em."

"You might hear some gripin' from Jug or Rudy, but not from the other two," Milhauser said mildly. He unlocked the cellblock entrance and picked up the tray. "Nice seein' you again, Mister Dent."

"What's so special about that Valentine jasper and his sidekick?" Moss challenged.

"Didn't mean they're special, Sheriff," shrugged Milhauser. "They're reasonable, that's all. Ain't apt to complain if breakfast is late."

At Moss' mention of Larry's name,

79

Dent had darted a quick glance to the open cellblock door. He was about to voice a question after Milhauser moved into the jailhouse, but Moss beat him to it with a question of his own.

"What makes you think any of them jail-breakers'd head for Alvison, anyway?"

In simple terms, the newspaperman confided his fears for Judge Blake's safety and the reason for those fears, the fact that all five were convicted murderers sentenced by Blake during his circuit-riding years, the fact that they had made threats against the judge. So much for his good intentions. Both lawmen scoffed at him.

"They wouldn't have the nerve," chuckled Prince.

"Blowhards," Moss said brusquely. "Damn near every killer pullin' a life sentence has shot off his mouth at the judge that sentenced him. Then, after their first year in a big pen, they forget him. Their spirit get's broken fast, Dent, in them territorial prisons."

Dent controlled his temper. To press the point would be futile; he understood Moss and his cousin and expected no better of them. Milhauser now lounged in the cellblock doorway, the empty tray tucked under an arm.

"Did you hear, Dutch?" asked Dent.

"Yeah, sure," nodded Milhauser. "And I'll be takin' another look at that bulletin, Mister Dent. The pictures too."

"Oh, they'll rue the day they show their faces in Alvison, them runaways," grinned Prince. "Old dead-Eye Milhauser'll give 'em hell."

No comment from Milhauser; since the bank robbery, he had become the town's most withdrawn citizen, and the most patient.

"What happened to your face, Deputy Prince?" Dent now enquired.

Prince's grin was swiftly erased. He muttered a curse.

"Don't worry about it, Jesse," soothed Moss. "Them Texans got nothin' but trouble waitin' for 'em."

"A man named Valentine — and who else?" prodded Dent.

"Henderson," shrugged Prince.

"No," said Moss. "Allison."

"Emerson," offered Milhauser.

"Who asked *you*?" challenged Moss.

"Well . . . " Dent shrugged casually as he got to his feet. "Couple strangers in jail are always interesting. Anybody mind if I look them over?" He spread his hands. "You know I never carry a weapon, Sheriff, but search me if you wish. And Dutch needn't let me into their cells. I can talk from the passage."

"They're no-accounts!" snorted Moss. "Ten cents' worth of trail-trash. But, if you're all that curious . . . " He jerked a thumb, "help yourself."

The editor won a cheery welcome after entering the jail. Jug Updike asked if he happened to have a bottle on his person. Rudy Lucas urged him to attend court this afternoon.

"And fetch somethin' to write on, Mister Dent."

"Big story for me, Rudy?" grinned Dent.

"I plan on conductin' my own defense — so how d'you like that?" bragged the compulsive thief.

"Got to say I admire your courage, Rudy," declared Dent. "With Casper Edmunds prosecuting, I mean. A hard man to beat, Rudy."

"I got faith," Lucas assured him. "The Lord protects the righteous — and them that's unjustly accused."

"If you're countin' on divine intervention," advised Dent, "you'd better get down on your knees."

"After I'm through eatin' this swill — maybe," said Lucas.

Dent leaned against the bars of the cell housing the Texans and greeted them cordially. The greeting wasn't returned. They squatted on their bunks, eating the austere oatmeal cooked by Milhauser, not enjoying it, just eating automatically. Dent was at once reminded of the notorious trouble-shooters' legendary distrust of the press, an emotion as deep-rooted as their hostility toward the lawless.

"I'm not here to request an interview," he offered.

"That'll save all three of us some time," growled Stretch.

"Just thought I'd look you over," shrugged Dent. "You must have arrived quietly. I honestly didn't know you were here. By the way, did you happen to hear about the breakout from Bormann, the territorial prison?"

"Haven't heard," grunted Larry. "Ain't interested."

"Well, *I* certainly am," said Dent. "Biggest breakout in the history of this territory, better than seventy, according to the Bormann authorities. Only five still at large. Five killers."

"We supposed to care a damn?" challenged Stretch.

"By now, you've heard of Judge Blake," guessed Dent. "He'll be presiding at your trial."

"So we've heard of Judge Blake," shrugged Larry.

"By coincidence, he was the presiding judge at their trials, those same five uncaptured killers," said Dent. "Five bad ones in five different towns. And they all made the same threat after the judge pased sentence. They'd break out some day. They'd track him down — and kill him."

"Runt, you listenin' to any of this?" asked Stretch.

"Nary a word," said Larry.

"Sheriff Moss doesn't think it likely any of them will reach Alvison," offered Dent. "I hope he's right." He nodded affably. "And that's all I wanted to say."

Convinced his friend was a marked man, but doubting there was any immediate danger, Dent deliberately postponed his visit to the Blake home until 10 a.m. Phoebe Blake, a young lady dedicated to a regular routine, was wont to serve coffee at that precise hour. Lou Dent made fine coffee, but Phoebe's was the best the Sentinel editor had ever tasted.

At exactly 9.55 he paid his call at the well-tended double story abode on Mailey Street and was admitted by the judge's daughter. Phoebe had blossomed into appealing womanhood, a slender blonde of pleasing countenance and expressive blue eyes.

"Mister Dent! A pleasure as always. Dad will be glad to see you." She closed the door, linked arms with him and walked him toward the ground floor parlor. "You're our second visitor this morning. Ross looked in a few moments ago."

"Your devoted suitor," grinned Dent. "Well, you're at that happy time of your young life, Phoebe honey. The courting period. Enjoy it while you may."

"It's nice to be popular," she smiled. "But, really, I'm in no hurry. Marriage can wait." She ushered him into the parlor. "Dad — Ross — more company."

"And most welcome." From where he sat, Judge Orin Blake raised a blue-veined hand in greeting. He was looking gaunt nowadays, his cheekbones more pronounced, but still impressive in his own quiet way. The mane of iron-grey hair was well-barbered, the mustache and spade beard neatly clipped. "Good to see you, Roy. You here for the pleasure of my company, Phoebe's coffee, or both?"

"Both," said Dent. "'Morning, Orin. And you, Mister Gregory."

The suave attorney rose to shake his hand. Ross Gregory, the handsomest of Alvison's three resident lawyers, was also the most ambitious. Bound to succeed, locals opined. Headed for big things, Ross Gregory. By the time Wyoming reached statehood, this up-and-at-'em attorney would probably be a candidate for state governor, so folks said. He was dark-haired with clean-cut features and ingratiating demeanor; he patronized the town's most expensive tailor.

"You're well, I trust, Mister Dent?" he courteously enquired. "Your charming wife also?"

"Quite well," nodded Dent. "I'll be sure to tell her you asked."

"Well now," beamed Phoebe. "By happy coincidence, I was about to serve coffee."

"Serve Roy's and mine in my study," her father suggested, as he began the effort to rise. "You young people would prefer to be together, I'm sure, and instinct tells me Roy's here for a private discussion with me."

As he moved across to help his friend from the chair, Dent remarked very seriously,

"That's quite an instinct you have — did I ever tell you? This talent for sensing a man's need to consult with you. You're good at it, Orin. Very good."

"Either I'm uncommonly intuitive," Blake said good-humoredly, "or you're transparent, an easy man to read."

Dent helped him fit his crutches into position and, as the judge nodded so-long to Gregory and started for the doorway, followed along.

"With you in a moment, Ross," called Phoebe, hurrying away to the kitchen.

In Blake's study, a few minutes later, the old friends sipped coffee and got to talking, Blake as comfortable as he could hope to be in the padded chair behind the desk, Dent seated beside him.

"New treatment any help?" the newspaperman asked.

"I'm sure young Doctor Howland is better qualified to handle an arthritis case," shrugged Blake. "That's no reflection on Phin Corkhill of course. You know how I feel about Phin."

"Who could dislike that old healer?" grinned Dent. "All caught up in his favorite subject. Why can't some of us be six-footers?"

"Why are there the short, the tall and the in-betweens?" Blake chuckled indulgently. "To me, it doesn't seem important. Still, if the old fellow derives pleasure from what he calls his research, where's the harm? As for young

Howland, I'm sure he's doing his best, but I don't hope for miracles, Roy."

"Too bad you have to contend with so much pain," frowned Dent.

"I'm resigned to it," Blake confided. "Better for Phoebe if I discipline myself against grouching. Nothing to be gained by distressing her. And now what's on your mind?"

"The Bormann affair," said Dent.

"Bad business," mused Blake. "Heavy casualties I believe. Guards as well as escapees. But the search parties . . . "

"Recaptured all but five, last I heard," said Dent.

"The hunt will continue," opined Blake. "Five you say? Well, they'll be apprehended soon enough."

"That's my fervent hope, old friend," muttered Dent.

"Something I should know?" demanded Blake.

"Lifers, all five of them," said Dent. "I'll name them and you'll remember them. You should, Orin. You passed sentence on them. Every man a convicted murderer. And they threatened you."

"I've been threatened so often . . . " Blake grinned mirthlessly, "I've lost count, Roy. Some accept my ruling calmly. Some — but not many. A man facing the prospect of spending the rest of his life in prison — he'd have to resent it. If you feel you should name these men, go ahead." He listened intently to Dent's list of the names. Then, nodding slowly, he assured him, "I've not forgotten them."

"Death threats, Orin," warned Dent. "And Bormann is not exactly a million miles from here."

"Doesn't seem possible they could reach Alvison, get close enough for an attempt on my life," said Blake. "You've alerted the sheriff?"

"I felt that was the least I owe you," said Dent.

"Owe me?" frowned Blake. "Why should you feel any responsibility?"

"Orin, my paper circulates far and wide," said Dent. "Court reports are published regularly, the name of Alvison's judge always rating a mention along with prosecutor and defense counsel. If Melville or the others don't already know where to find you, they could easily find out. They need only happen on an old edition of the Sentinel."

"Maybe so," nodded Blake. "But yours is not the only paper in which my name has been mentioned. Relax, my friend. Next thing we know, you'll be developing a guilt complex."

"I don't want to be an alarmist," shrugged Dent. "By now, they could be on their way back to Bormann under heavy escort. It's just . . . "

"Yes," said Blake. "Some of them — Melville, Thane and Alton for instance — are of above-average intelligence."

"Many a lawman would say those five should have been hanged," Dent pointed out. "They're killers after all."

"I know you think I'm too much the idealist," Blake said sadly. "Possibly a little squeamish?"

"Well . . . " began Dent.

"It's not all that easy, pronouncing sentence of death," declared Blake. "Those I've sent to the gallows deserved the supreme penalty, I know, but it was never easy for me. And a lawman might argue hanging is too merciful a fate for a conscienceless murderer. It's a complex question, Roy, and one I prefer not to discuss."

"As you wish, Orin," said Dent.

They dropped the subject of capital punishment and talked of other matters. All personal conversation was off the record; on this mutual understanding, they had become firm friends. Rarely was Judge Blake quoted in the Sentinel, and then only with his permission. By adhering to this practice, Dent had won his trust, which he valued.

In the parlor, meanwhile, Phoebe was expressing surprise that her gentleman caller would not appear in court this afternoon.

"Four cases, Ross? And you aren't

acting for any of them?"

"I have more important briefs to study," drawled Gregory. "Why waste my time on our local sneak-thief? I'm told Rudy Lucas will conduct his own defence this time. As for Jug Updike, what defense can one offer for the town drunk? And those roughneck strangers, an assault and battery case, poor Warren is welcome to it."

"Warren's appearing today?" she asked eagerly.

"I could have handled it, I suppose," he shrugged. "But I declined for his sake." He smiled blandly. "You see? I'm genuinely sorry for my rival."

"Very generous of you," sniffed Phoebe.

"No, honestly," he assured her. "I like Warren. And the fact that *you* like him causes me no qualms. You're a level-headed young woman, Phoebe my dear. Haven't I always said as much? Too much the realist to let your emotions get the better of you. Warren is the typical lame duck and

94

you feel sorry for him. Well, so do I. Poor fellow must be down to his last few dollars, desperately needs whatever fee those brawlers can afford. That's why I let him take their case."

"I think you and Mister Edmunds are much too hard on Warren," she chided.

"We don't mean to be," he grinned. "But it's so obvious to us. I'm sure it must be just as obvious to you and to the judge, though, of course, a gentleman of his discretion would never comment . . . "

"*What* is obvious?" demanded Phoebe.

"Why, that poor Warren chose the wrong profession," said Gregory. "He doesn't have what it takes, my dear. No confidence at all. Casper Edmunds has him intimidated. At the vaguest hint of a counter-argument from old Casper, he comes apart at the seams. Too self-conscious for his own good, our friend Warren. Too diffident. His life seems to be one long apology."

"I'm sorry for Warren," she frowned.

"But I doubt I'd let my natural sympathy affect my reasoning."

"Very wise," he said approvingly. "Since your mother's death, you have tied yourself to your father. Because of his disability, I mean. You shouldn't make the same mistake with Warren. Lame ducks, my dear, are poor husband material."

Brilliant attorney though he was, an up-coming lawyer with a fine mind, it never occurred to Ross Gregory that he had inserted his well-shod foot into his smiling mouth. From her parents Phoebe had inherited intelligence and sensitivity. Lame duck. An unfortunate choice of words. Unforgiveable in fact. She wondered, while farewelling Gregory at the front door a short time later, if sheepish, awkward Warren were capable of such a boner, even in his most inept moments.

It had been an historic visit, had Gregory but realized as much.

At 1 p.m., when Jacob Falstead made his unobtrusive entrance on the Alvison scene, the Texans had finished an indifferent lunch and were shaving; unlike Jug and Rudy, they were mutually agreed they should make themselves presentable for their appearance before Judge Blake; well, they could do their best with the material on which they had to work.

Now, while drawing his razor over his lantern jaw, Stretch finally deigned to recall the editor of the Alvison paper.

"That scribbler-hombre — Dent? What d'you make of all his palaver about some jailbreaker cravin' to massacree this Judge Blake?"

"I don't make anything of it, because I don't care a damn," growled Larry, wiping his razor. "Let Fat-Gut Moss and his deputies take care of any killer tries to gun the judge. All I want is Rober."

"We never did take kindly to cardsharps," Stretch mildly remarked. "How much did he take us for?"

"Three hundred, the hog's share of

"our bankroll," said Larry.

"We've lost more'n that in our day," mused Stretch.

"It ain't how much he sharped from me that matters," countered Larry. "If he only gypped me for a lousy ten bucks, I'd still have to square accounts with him. I just ain't partial to cheaters."

"You and me both," shrugged Stretch.

"No matter how long it takes, no matter how long we got to stick in this town," declared Larry, "we ain't leavin' till that three hundred is back in my wallet. Let that sonofabitch get away with it? *That'll* be the day."

"You'll get your chance, runt," Stretch said comfortingly. "You'll think of somethin'."

By 1.30 p.m., having heard that Judge Blake would be holding court this day, Falstead positioned himself in the mouth of a side alley directly opposite the county courthouse. He was nursing the loaded rifle torn from a Bormann guard's grasp. The saddle-animal stolen from a homesteader was

98

tied in the back alley just around the rear corner of the building he now lounged against, Holmark's Bakery. He would, he assured himself, easily spot his target. Blake was obliged to use crutches nowadays and would therefore be conspicuous.

'I'd recognize you anyway, damn you,' he reflected, watching the first handful of people cross the street to enter the courthouse. 'Could I forget the self-righteous bastard sent me to Bormann — for the rest of my born days? Damn you, Judge Blake, this is gonna pleasure me — a whole lot!'

Five minutes later, he tensed to the feel of a hand on his shoulder. Somebody had sneaked up on him. He clenched his teeth and, assuming he had been recognized by a local lawman, was about to whirl and use the butt of his rifle when the familiar voice, soft and derisive, smote his ears.

"Well, well, well! Jake Falstead. Fancy meeting you here."

4

Weight of Evidence

THE burly man threw a quick glance over his shoulder and swore softly.

"Thane!"

"I've been here an hour," drawled Miles Thane. "You?"

"Got in one o'clock or thereabouts," shrugged Falstead.

He begged a smoke from the other escapee, lit up and looked him over. In the matter of apparel, Thane had fared well. Lean and venerable-looking, he wore a rumpled black suit, white shirt with celluloid collar and black string tie and his most reassuring expression, this ensemble topped off by a flat-brimmed black hat. A large bible was tucked under his left arm and, right now, his demeanor was matching the outfit; he looked the part, the typical itinerant preacher.

"Are we working together, Jake?" he enquired. "Or are you set on playing a lone hand?"

"Take your best shot — after you find another stakeout," was Falstead's gruff reply.

"Better that way," decided Thane. "If our luck holds, your slug will hit him about the same time as mine." He smiled his gentle smile and confided, "I'd as soon be close anyway. Something I've been promising myself for near six years. To be close enough to see his face when he feels my bullet tearing through him." He studied the facade of the courthouse a moment, glanced along the alley. "Your choice, Jake, this alleymouth? I've seen better stakeouts. Wide open, don't you think?"

"I won't make my play from here," muttered Falstead. "Already took a look." He jerked a thumb. "The baker. Workin' all by himself. And nary a customer since I got here."

"Just so I won't foul up your routine," said Thane. "Did you plan on doing it when he arrives, or when court adjourns?"

"I'll likely wait till he's through," said Falstead.

"Exactly what I had in mind," grinned Thane. "I'll come out when the courthouse empties, wait for him to show, and . . . "

"Me too," nodded Falstead. "So-long, Reverend."

"Bless you, brother."

Thane flashed the bulky man a satirical smile, moved out of the alley and was sauntering the east sidewalk when, at 1.50, Deputy Milhauser drove the converted army ambulance with the barred windows up Main toward the courthouse with Moss and Prince riding escort. Locals drew close to watch the manacled prisoners taken from the vehicle and hustled through the main entrance. The crowd then began filing in and, a few minutes later, Judge Blake's surrey rolled into view, his daughter driving.

This handsome rig was stalled some 20 yards north of the courthouse. On street duty now, Milhauser was on hand to help Phoebe alight, then to assist her father. From two vantage-points, Falstead and Thane covertly studied the slow, awkward movements of the man they had sworn to kill. Struggling with his crutches, temporarily obscured by the attentive deputy, he was transfered from the rear seat with considerable difficulty. The portly, distinguished-looking Casper Edmunds then came on the scene to offer assistance and, grateful for the county prosecutor's help, Milhauser at last deposited the judge on the sidewalk, steadying himself on his crutches.

"Seems to become a little harder every time," Blake remarked with a rueful grin. "My thanks, Deputy. You too, Casper."

"He's so stubborn," complained Phoebe. "Just won't listen to Doctor

103

Howland. Really, Dad, a wheelchair would make everything so much easier."

"You'd be more mobile, Orin," Edmunds opined.

"When I can no longer manage crutches, it will have to be a wheelchair," muttered Blake. "Until then, crutches it will be. And now we'd best get inside. Thanks again, Deputy."

By the time the judge entered the courtroom with his daughter and prosecutor Edmunds, every seat provided for the public was occupied. The usual Alvison crowd was in attendance, interested parties, disinterested parties with nothing better to do, layabouts, old timers seeking a diversion from their regular routine of whittling and gossiping outside the town's livery stables and barber shops. Neeley Rober and his hangers-on were well to the fore, Sheriff Moss standing before the bench and keeping a wary eye on the crowd, Deputy Prince standing over the defendants. Their manacles removed, Larry, Stretch, Lucas and Updike sat in the front row while the two lawyers occupied a nearby table, Edmunds with arms folded and face impassive, Warren Kipp fussing with his notes, looking flustered already.

With help from Phoebe, Blake reached his seat on the bench and lowered himself into it. She set his crutches against his chair and retreated to a seat on the dais. Moss then traded nods with Blake and threateningly announced that the court of Alvison County was now in session, Judge Orin Blake presiding.

"So here we go again," Stretch quietly remarked to Larry.

"No talkin'!" rasped Prince.

Blake cleared his throat and began.

"Let's start with an old acquaintance, Sheriff Moss."

"Thadeus Updike," announced Moss. "The charge bein' drunkenness in a house of worship, namely the Methodist chapel on South Colton Street, from which the accused was removed by Deputy Prince."

"On your feet," Prince ordered the barfly.

Updike was at once upstanding, nodding cheerily to Blake.

"'Afternoon, Judge."

"You ain't here to howdy the judge," chided Moss. "How do you plead?"

"Guilty, Judge," grinned Upduke.

"Have you anything to say, Jug, before I pass sentence?" asked Blake.

"Like to say the church was empty when I sneaked in there, Judge," Updike said virtuously. "I had a load on, sure, and I was needin' to sleep it off, but you know I'd never show disrespect by stumblin' in there while Reverend O'Donnell's conductin' services."

"I think you mean Reverend Tyson," Blake gently corrected. "Father O'Donnell is at the Catholic church on Sycamore Road."

"'Scuse me," apologized the defendant. "I keep gettin' all them holy places mixed up, you know?"

"Why a church, Jug?" frowned Blake.

"Better'n a saloon," explained Updike. "Man can't get no sleep in a saloon. Too much noise."

"Have you finished?" prodded Blake.

"Like to say I didn't resist arrest," offered Updike. "I mean, I never give these badge-toters no trouble. Specially Jesse Prince, on account of him packin' that purty pistol of his and bein' trigger-happy and all."

"Hey now, Judge, he's got no right to . . . !" began Moss.

"Confine yourself to direct answers, Jug," advised Blake. Before passing sentence, he waxed curious and put a last question to the accused. "Jug, I've lost count of your appearances in this court, and always on the same charge. Why do you drink all the time?"

"I like booze," grinned Updike,

A burst of laughter from the body of the court was quelled by two raps of Blake's gavel. Then, with a half-smile, he passed sentence.

"Seven days in the county jail. The prisoner is returned to custody." As

Updike resumed his chair, he nodded to Moss. "Next case?"

"A charge of theft against Rudolph Adamson Lucas," intoned Moss.

"And the stolen article?" asked Blake.

"One hammer," declared Moss. "Purloined from the premises of Mister Lloyd Carbro, undertaker."

"Your Honor, I appear for the plaintiff in this action," said Edmunds rising. "I believe the matter can be disposed of quickly, I see no need for an opening address. My client, Mister Carbro, will testify to the essential facts."

Fixing a kindly eye on the younger lawyer, Blake enquired,

"You're appearing for the accused, Mister Kipp?"

"No — I mean — if it please the court . . . " Warren jerked upright, blushing in confusion as he bumped the table and sent half of his notes cascading to the floor. "Excuse me, Your Honor. This defendant — uh

— is not my client."

While he retrieved his scattered papers, the judge frowned at the second defendant, who rose and sternly announced,

"I'm conductin' my own defense, Judge, if it's okay by you."

Blake winced. Edmunds grimaced in exasperation.

"Mister Lucas, that is your right," said Blake. "But a defendant conducting his own case — without previous experience — is at a disadvantage. Also, I fear, apt to delay these proceedings."

"Don't you fret on my account, Judge," Lucas said confidently. "I won't be bendin' your ear, makin' no speeches. I'll just be askin' a couple of questions. And then, why, you can deliver your rulin' and I'll just walk out of here."

"Such confidence," smiled Edmunds.

"Proceed, Mister Edmunds," urged Blake. "And let's hope for the best.

A simple case of petty theft, according

to the prosecutor. He called the plaintiff to the stand and, having taken the oath, Carbro told of having sighted the defendant loitering in his workroom. At his challenge, the defendant had taken to his heels. Around the undertaker's premises he had been pursued to be apprehended in the rear yard by Carbro himself.

"He's the biggest thief in town. Everybody knows that. Why, he's been caught and found guilty in this very court and done more time in the county jail then even Jug Updike. There was a hammer missin' and I just knew he stole it, so I . . . !"

Edmunds wasn't required to discipline his witness. Blake did that, courteously but firmly, after which Carbro declared he had searched the accused and sent an employee to fetch the law. The defendant had then been placed under arrest by Deputy Prince.

"And the missing item, the hammer?" demanded Blake.

"We found it a couple days later,

Judge," growled Carbro. "In a corner of the yard. Right where he threw it. Before I caught up with him, you know?"

"No — I do not know," said Blake. "Mister Edmunds?"

"The prosecution rests, Your Honor," said Edmunds. "And, anticipating your reaction, let me say I do agree the evidence is circumstantial."

"Perhaps too much so," remarked Blake.

"Again, I'm forced to agree," nodded Edmunds.

"Hey, whose side are you on?" scowled Carbro.

"That's enough, Mister Carbro," chided Blake. "No, you may not step down." He eyed Lucas expectantly. "Cross-examination ?"

"If it please the court." Having faced charges on innumerable occasions, Rudy Lucas was up on procedure and feeling more than a little smug right now. To Blake's secret amusement, the accused rose and approached the witness-box with left thumb hooked in armhole of vest and right hand stroking his nose, an all-too-familiar characteristic, but not one of his own. Maybe unintentionally, maybe deliberately, he was aping the county prosecutor. "Yes, Judge, just a few questions and we'll be all through here. First question, Mister Carbro. Did you see me swipe your hammer?"

"It was hidden under your coat when I chased you out of . . . " began Carbro.

"You saw me stash a hammer under my coat?" challenged Lucas.

"Didn't have to see," snapped Carbro. "You made a run for it, so I knew you'd taken *somethin'*."

"Find anything of your own on me when you jumped me and searched me?" demanded Lucas.

"No — because you threw that hammer away just before . . . "

"You see me throw it away?"

"I damn well know for a fact . . . !"

The judge intervened at this point and, as well as warning the witness against harsh language, reminded him he was under oath. He then glanced at Edmunds.

"I trust, Mister Edmunds, the plaintiff fully understands the significance of giving evidence under oath?"

"I'm sure he realizes he must confine himself to the truth and refrain from speculation, Your Honor," said Edmunds. "At least . . . " He stared hard at the witness, "I certainly hope so."

"Mister Carbro . . . " began Blake.

"I'm not through with him, Judge," grinned Lucas.

"My apologies for interrupting your cross-examination," Blake said dryly.

"Well, that's okay," shrugged Lucas. "Go right ahead."

"It is obvious to me," Blake told Carbro, "that you gave Mister Edmunds the impression you'd actually witnessed the crime of which you have accused the defendant."

"Well — uh . . . "

"I'm sure Mister Edmunds conferred

with you at some length."

"Well, sure."

"And you did give that impression?"

"I guess so."

"A false statement under oath renders you liable to a charge of perjury," warned Blake. "Is that quite clear?" Carbro nodded sullenly. "So I now ask you did you at any time see the stolen item in the defendant's possession?"

Carbro clench his teeth.

"I guess I didn't."

"Yes or no?"

"No."

Blake shrugged impatiently.

"Then there is no case against the defendant. Theft, you must understand, has to be proven. Justice never assumes, Mister Carbro. The defendant's previous convictions warrant only limited consideration. Every accusation has to be substantiated, and you have admitted you cannot support this particular charge with positive evidence. Therefore I've no choice but to dismiss the charge and order the defendant's release from custody."

"That's tellin' 'em, Judge!" chuckled Lucas.

"You may leave the court," sighed Blake.

"That for you, Lloyd Carbro!" gloated Lucas, snapping his fingers.

"I said . . . " Blake patiently repeated, "You may leave."

"On my way, Judge, on my way!" chortled Lucas.

"You may step down," Blake told Carbro, as Lucas strutted up the centre aisle to the entrance. "And now . . . ?"

"On your feet, you two," Prince rasped at the Texans.

Poker-faced, the drifters rose to listen to the charges announced by the sheriff. The accused, Lawrence Valentine and Woodville Emerson, according to the plaintiffs, had indulged themselves in an orgy of assault, battery and riotous behavior in one of Alvison's most popular houses of entertainment, namely the Palace of Joy. After this, they were allowed to resume their seats. Warren apologetically informed the judge he was appearing for the defendants. It having been ascertained the accused were waiving the right to trial by jury, Edmunds then delivered his opening address, an impassioned, indignant denouncement of 'these shiftless vagabonds who so wantonly disturbed the peace of Alvison, who attacked a respected businessman of this town, also six of his employees . . . '

Worse, far worse, the accused Valentine had savagely assaulted an officer of the law, namely Deputy Jesse Prince.

"Such brutality cannot go unpunished, Your Honor," Edmunds declared in conclusion. "The county will press for the heaviest penalty in this case. An example must be set. Today, having attained the status of a well-ordered, peace-loving community, Alvison must be protected against outrages of this kind. And stiff sentences are the obvious deterrent."

He nodded encouragingly to the plaintiffs and called his first witness. Neeley Rober took the stand, was sworn in and, at Edmunds' urging, delivered his well-rehearsed lies. He had assumed the defendant Valentine to be harmless enough at the time of inviting him to join his poker party. Later, however, Valentine proved himself a sore loser and no gentleman, actually accusing him of cheating. Not content with that, he had kicked him out of his chair after throwing whiskey into his face. Mister Edward Brinley, a sporting gentleman of good reputation, had attempted to restrain Valentine from further violence, only to be brutally assaulted.

"Realizing Valentine had lost control of himself, I ordered two of my employees to remove him from the premises . . . "

"Their names, if you please," prodded Edmunds.

"Peter Cratchley and Horace Dagget," said Rober. "They tend bar at my place."

The lies continued. As well as attacking the barkeeps, Valentine had vent his spleen on Ansell McWhirter. His friend, the other defendant, had then attacked three other employees of the Palace, Messrs Heinz, Pooley and Daniels, the dice, faro and roulette supervisors respectively.

"And the attack on Deputy Prince?" asked Edmunds.

"There was some confusion by the time that incident occurred, and I had no clear view of it," said Rober.

"No more questions, Your Honor," nodded Edmunds. He turned to smile benevolently at the painfully self-conscious Warren. "Your witness, Mister Kipp."

Slowly, cautiously, Warren approached the witness box; he made it without tripping, but was still nervous when he put his first question.

"It is true, is it not, Mister Rober, that dissatisfied patrons have been ejected from your establishment on numerous occasions?"

"These things happen," shrugged Rober. "But, of course, it's always handled discreetly, usually by Mister McWhirter."

"And the cause of these disturbances?" prodded Warren.

"Drunk and disorderly, pestering other patrons, making too free with my female employees." Rober shrugged again. "That kind of thing."

"No other causes?" asked Warren. "Is Mister Valentine the first patron ever to have complained of being cheated?"

"Well, no," frowned Rober. "There have been others, but only a few. The Palace has a reputation for fair dealing. I run a square place, Counsellor. We never take advantage of men patronizing our games of chance. No cheating. That's our strict rule."

"Commendable, I'm sure," nodded Warren. "And, when Mister Valentine accused you of cheating him — to be precise, of having dealt yourself a card from under the deck — you denied the accusation?"

"Your Honor," said Edmunds, rising. "Witness has already testified to that effect. Is this repetition necessary?"

"Mister Kipp?" frowned Blake.

"I'll not pursue that question, Your Honor," said Warren. He adjusted his spectacles and eyed the witness intently. "Did you or did you not threaten my client, order him to keep his hands above the table and declared you were pointing a pistol at him — under the level of the tabletop?"

"Just a ruse, a vain attempt to discourage him from rash action," smiled Rober. "A bluff play. Of course I didn't have a pistol pointed at him."

"You did, however, so claim?"

"Well, yes, but . . . "

"And did you indeed deal a card to yourself from under the deck?"

"Objection!" growled Edmunds.

"On what grounds?" asked Blake.

"Mister Edmunds has already covered that point," declared Edmunds. "This repetition — really — my young colleague should know better."

"Any reprimands are my prerogative, Mister Edmunds," said Blake.

"Of course, Your Honor," nodded Edmunds.

"Mister Kipp . . . " began Blake.

"My apologies, Your Honor," mumbled Warren. "I withdraw the last question. And — uh — I have no more questions."

"He ain't doin' so good, runt," whispered Stretch.

"Give him time," shrugged Larry.

Came now the parade of other witnesses for the prosecution. Wisely, Edmunds did not call on Carbro until Brinley and Quill had backed up Rober's statement. None of these three could be intimidated by the ineffectual cross-examination of the defense counsel, and that went double for the barkeeps, the tablehands and the mountainous Anse McWhirter, all still showing the marks of their set-to with the defendants.

Deputy Prince, last to be called,

testified to having entered the saloon to investigate the disturbance. He had at once perceived a stranger, now identified as the defendant Valentine, reaching to his holster.

"Only one thing I could do," he gravely assured Edmunds. "He had to be discouraged — fast. I had no choice but to draw and fire at his gunarm."

"In all that confusion — men brawling — surely gunplay at short range was a drastic action?" suggested Edmunds. "You first called on the accused to desist, I take it?"

"I challenged him, sure," nodded Prince. "Couldn't make myself heard above all that din. The place was in uproar. So there was nothin' else I could do. But I knew there'd be no danger of my bullet hittin' anybody but Valentine. I'm a sure shot, sir."

At Edmunds' urging, he then recounted his being struck by a chair hurled by the defendant, seized by the defendant and hurled through the street-window.

"Your witness, Mister Kipp," offered Edmunds.

"Deputy, please rise," requested Warren, as he approached the witnesss box. Prince frowned at him as he obeyed. "Your badge of authority is clearly visible to me, Deputy. Right there on your vest."

"Right where I always wear it," nodded Prince. "Can I sit down now?"

"Sit down," invited Warren. "And tell the court if you were similarly attired when attacked by the defendant."

"Uh — what . . . ?" began Prince.

"You wore a coat last night — is that not so?" asked Warren.

"Well, I'm — uh — not sure about . . . " shrugged Prince.

"Deputy, you'd surely remember," interjected Blake.

"All right," said Prince, "A coat, yeah."

"Which concealed your badge?" prodded Warren.

"It might've," said Prince.

"You have told us you took aim at the

123

defendant's gunarm," Warren reminded him. "You're aware, I presume, that your bullet grazed his back?"

"He moved just as I triggered," muttered Prince. "But, listen, he was about to pull his gun, nothin' surer."

"No more questions," said Warren.

As Prince quit the stand, Blake called on Warren to make his opening address.

"And take your time, Mister Kipp," he said encouragingly. "You seem nervous, but you shouldn't be."

Warren's opening address lasted only a few moments. His great handicap, acute self-consciousness, was giving him hell; he was aware of Blake's sympathetic gaze and, though he lacked the nerve to glance her way, he was sure Phoebe's eyes were on him. As an orator, he was a minus quality. But his mind was well-disciplined now.

'Rely on your clients' shrewdness,' he advised himself. 'Put your faith in Doctor Corkhill's popularity. Don't try to impress Judge Blake with rhetoric.

That's Casper Edmunds' strong point, not yours.'

His brief address added up to no more than an assurance that he would prove prejudice and a reasonable doubt as to the accuracy of the evidence offered by prosecution witnesses.

"That's all, Mister Kipp?" asked Blake. "Very well. Call your first witness."

"I call the defendant, Lawrence Valentine," said Warren.

As Larry stirred, Stretch nudged him urgently and begged, "Stay cool, runt."

Larry rose, moved to the stand and was sworn in by Moss. His face turned toward the Rober faction as he seated himself, and then he was trading stares with Warren, listening to his question.

"Despite last night's violent activity and the wound you sustained, do you have a clear memory of all that transpired from the time of your arrival at the Palace of Joy with your friend, the co-defendant?"

"Real clear," nodded Larry. "I

haven't forgotten a thing."

"You were separated from your friend soon after entering the barroom?"

"Rightaway. He met up with Doc Corkhill while I joined the poker party."

"Was that your intention in visiting Mister Rober's saloon?"

"No. He invited me."

"Will you now tell the court how the dispute began?"

Larry told it detail by detail, beginning with Rober's trick deal, his challenge, then Rober's denial and threat.

"Did you actually see a pistol pointed at you by Mister Rober?" asked Warren.

"No," said Larry.

"So, as Mister Rober has testified, he could have been bluffing," Warren suggested.

"Could've been," agreed Larry. "But, when a man claims he's holding a gun on me, I'most always take his word for it."

"Please tell us how you reacted to

this threat," said Warren.

"With my right boot and a shot of whiskey," said Larry. "When I kicked at him, I heard somethin' hit the floor, then I threw the booze in his face, the tinhorn clobbered me, I gave him my elbow and, from then on . . . " He shrugged nonchalantly, "I was kept kind of busy."

"The plaintiffs, Messrs Cratchley and Dagget attempted to restrain you?"

"If you mean the barkeeps, Rober holered for'em and they jumped me."

"Meaning they attacked you?"

"Meanin' just that."

"Having — uh — defended yourself against the bartenders — what then?"

"The bouncer tried crowdin' me."

"So — again — you defended yourself?"

"It seemed like a good idea."

"Mister Valentine, did you at any time attempt to draw your revolver?" demanded Warren.

Grim-faced, Larry assured him,

"In that kind of set-up, I'd never

pull a gun. Only a trigger-happy jackass goes to shootin' in a crowded saloon."

"When shot by Deputy Prince, were you aware of his identity?"

"We'd only been in town a little while. Wasn't time for us to meet the local law."

"You did hurl a chair at the deputy?"

"Hit him with a chair, sure. Didn't know he was a lawman — couldn't see under his coat." Larry turned slightly, fixing a cold eye on the scowling Prince. "All I knew was I'd been shot from behind. When I turned, all I saw was a dude with a smokin' Colt in his fist. And I ain't denyin' I got good and mad."

"Objection, Your Honor!" Edmunds rose angrily. "my young colleague is encouraging the defendant to brag. His personal reactions are irrelevant to . . . "

"Over-ruled, Mister Edmunds," countered Blake. "We are dealing with the defendant's reaction to his suffering a gunshot wound. There *is* relevancy. Sudden pain and shock, Mister Edmunds. Obviously the cause of what followed."

"Very well," shrugged Edmunds.

"I beg your indulgence, Your Honor." Humbly, Warren confessed, "I have omited to establish a fact pertinent to my client's action . . . "

"You wish to revert to a previous question?" asked Blake.

"If I may," nodded Warren.

"Then do so," urged Blake.

"Was anger and shock your only motive for throwing a chair at Deputy Prince?" prodded Warren.

"I had a better reason," declared Larry. "He was re-cockin' that fancy six-shooter."

"You feared he would fire again?" challenged Warren.

"He was thumbin' the hammer back, and I wasn't about to take a chance," Larry said bluntly. "So I used the chair to slow him down. I was still hurtin', still good and mad, and I guess that's why I hurled him through a window."

Warren nodded absently, turned away and muttered,

"Cross-examine, Mister Edmunds?"

Edmunds rose, hooked a thumb in his vest, stroked his nose and advanced on Larry with eyes gleaming.

"Now it comes," Rober confidently remarked to Brinley. "That fool Kipp's trying to make me look bad, but now . . ."

"What's happened to Kipp?" wondered the gambler. "He never showed as much nerve before."

"That muscle-bound Texan is headed for a territorial pen," grinned Rober. "Him and his skinny sidekick. When old Casper gets through with Valentine, it won't be *me* looks bad."

"In the body of the court, Roy Dent cocked an expectant ear and leaned forward, pencil poised over his own notebook. Just as keenly interested was the aged but zesty Dr Phineas Corkhill. Soon enough, he would be testifying for the defense.

And with great pleasure.

5

The Decision

USUALLY, the steely eye and accusing demeanor of Casper Edmunds could be relied upon to intimidate, to thoroughly cower the most obstinate witnesses. With Larry, Edmunds found himself up against a tougher proposition. His first mistake was to chide Larry for maligning the characters of the prosecution witnesses. Did the defendant expect this court to believe Mister Rober and his associates had lied under oath? To this, Larry calmly replied,

"What this court believes is up to this court. I only believe what I see, and I saw Rober's trick deal. As for the other poker-players, maybe they didn't see Rober cheat. And maybe they ain't friends of his. Maybe he never saw 'em before."

"Your Honor, I strongly protest . . . !" began Edmunds.

"And rightly so," nodded Blake. "The witness will confine himself to direct answers. Proceed."

"I put it to you that, having lost more than you could afford, you also lost your temper," growled Edmunds. "Was Mister Rober not justified in using the term 'sore loser'?"

"I was down three hundred dollars," said Larry. "I've lost double that much — and more — and it didn't bother me any. It's a gamble after all. If losin' angers a man, he oughtn't gamble. And I gamble often. When you challenge a crooked dealer, he'll 'most always call you sore loser."

"Do you still insist you were struck by Mister Brinley?" demanded Edmunds.

"Right," nodded Larry.

"And the other victims of your brutality, the bartenders, the table supervisors and Mister McWhirter, do you still claim you allowed them to strike the first blows?" Edmunds smiled derisively. "A little far-fetched, wouldn't you say?"

"Might seem that way, but that's what we always do, my friend and I," shrugged Larry. "You have to understand we've run into this kind of trouble before. Any time some hard case tries crowdin' us, sure, we wait for him to swing on us before we hit back. That makes it self-defense, you know?"

"Self-defense indeed!" thundered Edmunds. "Six men beaten senseless — a respected law officer of this county hurled through a window . . . !"

"Excuse me, Your Honor." Warren stood up to timidly enquire, "Is my distinguished opponent questioning my client — or delivering another address for the prosecution?"

"Touché, Mister Kipp," Edmunds deigned to acknowledge.

"No speeches at this time, Mister Edmunds," cautioned Blake. "Direct questioning, if you please."

In vain, Edmunds fired challenges at Larry for another ten minutes. Larry was then permitted to stand down and Phineas Corkhill called to give his testimony. Already uneasy at Edmunds' failure to intimidate Larry, Rober became even more dismayed. None of his regular customers would have dared testify for the defense — none but the unpredictable elder healer, a neutral with no axe to grind.

Warren began by asking, with all due diplomacy, how a gentleman of such meagre stature had managed to follow every detail of the brawl at the Palace of Joy. Doc cheerfully explained he had climbed onto a table and was accorded good humored applause which had to be subdued by the judge's gavel.

"You were seated some distance from the table at which the dispute began?" asked Warren.

"But in sight of it," said Doc. "However, it was my guest, Mister Emerson, who first sensed — uh — impending violence."

"Objection, Your Honor," protested Edmunds. "Doctor Corkhill had barely become acquainted with the defendant Emerson and can hardly claim to have read his mind."

"Sustained," said Blake. "Mr. Warren, your witness should re-phrase his reply."

"Certainly," nodded Doc. "Would this be satisfactory? The second defendant was watching his friend, the first defendant. He must have anticipated trouble because he remarked, and I quote, 'I don't like the way my partner looks.' He then said, 'I'd best get over there.' But he never reached the poker table. By the time I'd mounted a table, Mister Emerson was being intercepted by three members of the saloon's staff." He gestured to the plaintiffs. "Specifically, those three showing severe facial bruises."

"And you saw . . . ?" prodded Warren.

"Both defendants repulsing assailants," said Doc. "Mister Valentine dealt with the bartenders — very effectively, may I say . . . "

"You may not, Doctor," Blake chided with his hand covering his mouth. "Answers, please. A clear statement of what you saw, but without comments."

"While Mister Valentine dealt with the bartenders, also the bouncer," offered Doc, "Mister Emerson defended himself against the three I've already mentioned. May I emphasize *defended* himself? He was most certainly resisting attack."

"Were you also a witness to the shooting?" asked Warren.

"At the sound of the shot, I naturally transferred my attention to the shooter," said Doc. "This much I clearly recall. Deputy Prince's badge could not be seen. His coat concealed it. And he was still aiming that — uh — rather distinctive pistol at Mister Valentine when Mister Valentine hurled a chair at him."

"A point not yet raised," frowned

Warren. "You saw Sheriff Moss and Deputy Milhauser enter the saloon — and arrest the defendants?"

"I did," said Doc.

"Did they submit peaceably?"

"Oh, yes. Just removed their sidearms and handed them to Deputy Milhauser."

"Cross-examination, Mister Edmunds?" offered Warren.

"Afternoon, Casper." Doc grinned and nodded.

Edmunds did consider the advisability of cross-examining the popular medico, but only for a moment. He shook his head.

"No questions, Your Honor. If you wish, and if there are no more witnesses for the defense, I am ready to deliver my closing address."

"Mister Kipp?" asked Blake.

"That concludes the case for . . ." began Warren.

"By your leave, your Honor." Roy Dent rose and gestured apologetically. "This is irregular and, until this moment, I had no intention of offering a statement."

"A statement, Mister Dent?" frowned Blake.

"I am peculiarly qualified to testify to the character and reputation of the defendants," explained Dent, "though I've never met them before this morning."

"I think Editor Dent should clarify that, Your Honor," frowned Edmunds. "My young colleague is obviously as surprised as I, so I assume he had no fore-knowledge of intervention by the press."

"I agree," nodded Blake. "Peculiarly qualified, Mister Dent?"

"Because of my profession, Your Honor," offered Dent. "Because these defendants have been accorded a great deal of publicity for all of twenty years. We of the press, you see, are familiar with their background, certain aspects of which are a matter of record."

"In newspaper offices," Edmunds said curtly.

"In a great many law offices,"

said Dent. "Also the files of the Pinkerton and Remington Detective Agencies, the Department of Justice, the Federal Marshal's headquarters and the U.S. Army. But it was not my intention to hold forth on what might be described as their trouble-shooting activities. I offer myself only as a character witness."

Trouble-shooters. Edmunds associated that term with bounty-hunting and the shady activities of freebooters taking the law into their own hands. The Sentinel editor, he decided, had played right into his hands.

"Your Honor, if you've no objection to Mister Dent's being heard . . . " he began.

"The character of the defendants does seem relevant to the matter at hand," reflected Blake. "Since the prosecution has been given every opportunity of attacking the character of strangers, perhaps it's only fair we should hear from a volunteer witness to whom they are not exactly strangers."

He stared hard at the newspaperman. "I take it you're willing to offer this information under oath, and that you realize Mister Edmunds may wish to contest your statements?"

"Yes, Your Honor," nodded Dent.

As he moved down the aisle, the Texans glanced his way and quietly traded comments.

"Are we gonna end up thankin' that scribbler?" Stretch wondered.

"Unless Mister Prosecutor throws him," mutter Larry. "Then we'll have *nothin'* to thank him for. Better he kept his mouth shut. Judges ain't partial to trouble-shooters."

After being sworn in by Moss, the newspaperman stressed aspects of the legend well-known to the press. Valentine was an expert poker-player. His talent for detecting a below-the-deck deal of a hideaway card was common knowledge. Neither Texan indulged in rash accusations. And, yes, they had seen the inside of many a frontier jail, had been arrested many times, usually as a result of their involvement in a pitched brawl. Ironically, they were never the aggressors. They did tend to permit their assailants the first blow in the invariably vain hope witnesses would support their claim of self-defense.

"Cardsharps and cattle-town rowdies are the lesser of their natural enemies, however," he pointed out. "These men have a deep-rooted hostility toward the bandit packs of the frontier. They are constantly at war with the lawless, admittedly on their own rough terms, and have been responsible for the apprehension of countless thieves and murderers. I make this statement voluntarily, believing the character of these men is vital to their defense in this case." He shrugged and added, "We of the press know them to be rough men, but not unreasonable and never irresponsible. That is all I have to say. Unless you have a question, Your Honor? Or you, Mister Edmunds?"

"Counsellor?" asked Blake.

"I will deal with Mister Dent's statement in my closing address," Edmunds decided.

His closing address built up to a tirade. After dismissing Dent's statement as reflecting the press' notorious talent for exaggerated eulogizing of unsavory frontier types, he insisted that the prosecution witnesses were men of good repute whose testimony must be believed. Valentine's testimony in his own defense was suspect, to say the least. And, with due respect for the estimable Doctor Corkhill, he was a man well past his prime. It was, therefore, reasonable to suspect his vision was defective, his eyesight not what it used to be, and that the hectic activity of the disturbance in the barroom could not have been accurately observed by a man of his advanced years.

Warren's closing address was shorter; by now he was overawed by the prosecutor's full-blown oratory.

"It should be apparent, Your Honor, that the testimony of the prosecution witnesses is heavily prejudiced. This is understandable, since the events under dispute occurred less than twenty-four hours ago. Feeling is still high and — uh — the plaintiffs still suffering the effects of the defendants' — uh — retaliatory action. I hesitate to even hint at perjury, but I respectfully suggest prejudice has clouded their memory of certain aspects of last night's unfortunate disturbance. By contrast, the testimony of Doctor Corkhill is perhaps a more accurate account of all that transpired. This testimony and the background information volunteered by Mister Dent clearly indicate that my clients were the victims rather than the instigators of this regrettable affair. Therefore, Your Honor, I plead for leniency for the defendants."

After Warren returned to his seat, silence prevailed for some 30 seconds. Blake didn't appear confused, just pensive. Edmunds, who knew him well, guessed the ruling would be delivered momentarily; it just didn't seem likely the judge would reserve his decision.

In the body of the court, locals were muttering among themselves, some discussing the case, some laying bets on the outcome. This subdued rumble ceased to the banging of Blake's gavel. He then delivered his decision.

"I find the testimony in this case too contradictory to justify a guilty verdict on all counts. In several areas, the defendants seem entitled to the benefit of the doubt. Though he has denied drawing a pistol on the defendant Valentine, the plaintiff Rober has admitted he did claim to have done so. The issue rests on one simple question. Were the defendants the aggressors, the instigators of last night's violence, or were they forced to defend themselves? Weighing the testimony of an observant non-combatant, Doctor Corkhill, against the testimony of men who were actually participants in what was obviously a hectic and confused melee, I find I must favor the defendants."

He used his gavel again to subdue the indignant protests of the Rober faction, then continued.

"As it seems obvious the defendant Valentine was unaware of Deputy Prince's official status, I dismiss the charge of assault on an officer of the law. The peace of this town was disturbed, however, and a great deal of turmoil created by the defendants. On the one hand, they were outnumbered. On the other hand . . . " He fixed a stern gaze on the Texans, "their retaliation was perhaps unnecessarily destructive. It is the judgement of this court that they be confined to the county jail for a further four days."

"But, damnitall . . . !" began Rober.

Moss was as furious as Rober, but his quick warning glance checked Rober's outburst.

"The prisoners are returned to custody of the sheriff," announced Blake. "This court is now adjourned."

When the first three locals came hustling out of the courthouse, Falstead sidled into the bakery and closed the street-door behind him. Baker Fritz Holmark, preoccupied until that moment with transferring pies from his oven to a table, looked up perplexedly. He was spare of physique; in the always heated atmosphere of the bakery there was little danger he would ever become overweight.

"You want something?" he asked. "Why'd you shut the door?"

"Stand right where you are and don't give me any fool arguments," scowled Falstead.

He picked up Holmark's 'Closed' sign and re-opened the door, but only long enough to hang it on the outside knob, and won a protest.

"Hey! You can't do that! I don't close up this time of day!"

Holmark's protests were cut short by

the stock of the rifle. He collapsed to the right of the oven. Falstead then positioned himself at the open front window, readied his rifle for action and kept his eyes on the people quitting the courthouse.

The two lawyers were among the last to emerge. They began moving off in different directions while a dozen or so townmen lingered atop the courthouse steps, awaiting the reappearance of Judge Blake and daughter. The three prisoners were ushered out by Moss and Prince, not manacled, but with six-guns prodding them. They were followed out by Blake, moving slowly on his crutches and with his daughter in attendance. A half-block north of the courthouse, Roy Dent and Doc Corkhill had encountered Deputy Milhauser and were pausing for a few friendly words.

"Move your butts," Moss harshly ordered the prisoners. "C'mon now! Down the steps to the wagon!"

"You sore about somethin', Sheriff

suh?" jibed Stretch, turning to grin at him.

His casual movement saved Orin Blake's life. The judge had paused to the left of the entrance and, with Phoebe steadying his left shoulder, was adjusting his right crutch. But Stretch wasn't noticing Blake or daughter. From the corner of his eye, he had glimpsed the furtive action of the black-garbed man emerging from the group at his right. A bible was tucked under the left arm. The right hand was drawing something from under the black coat, something at once recognized by the taller Texans.

The lawmen and their prodding Colts were forgotten. As well as loosing a warning yell, Stretch leapt at Thane. Blake and daughter froze and, at that moment, Falstead squeezed trigger. That harsh report echoed along Main and caused a scatter. At first startled, Moss and Prince suffered shock. The bullet sped past the sheriff's ear with only inches to spare. Blake and his daughter felt the airwind of it and heard the ugly thudding sound of the slug slamming into the facade of the courthouse, the bullet-hole appearing in the short space between their heads. Phoebe turned, stared aghast at the hole and promptly swooned, still clinging to her father's arm, pulling him with her as she collapsed.

The lawmen had reacted promptly after rallying from their shock. They dropped prone without thinking to order their prisoners to do likewise. Jug Updike wasn't waiting for an order anyway; he was down, huddled with his hands covering his head.

From a half-kneeling position, Larry darted one quick glance toward his partner before scanning the buildings opposite. Stretch had captured Thane's right wrist, but Thane was a struggling, cursing fanatic now, clawing for Stretch's face with his free hand. The last fleeing local vacated the area between the courthouse and the bakery when Larry spotted the rifle-barrel protruding.

From the uptown area, Milhauser was running toward the bakery with gun drawn.

Quickly, Larry bent over the quivering Moss, wrenched the Colt from his hand and thumbed back the hammer. He aimed and fired, his target the area just above the leveled rifle, just as Falstead's trigger-finger contracted. Inside the bakery, reviving at that moment, Fritz Holmark was witness to a harrowing sight, Falstead lurching backward from the impact of the .45 slug, the rifle discharging upward as he lost his grip of it. The stricken killer loosed one choking groan before crashing onto the laden table, mashing the pies lined there, his legs dangling grotesquely, arms outspread, eyes open and unseeing.

The second report caused the prone lawmen to flinch and Larry to turn quickly. Blake and Updike also saw Stretch break free of Thane, and Thane, right hand still gripping his hideaway pistol, blood staining his shirtfront, slumping to the top step.

"Get it away from him," urged Larry.

Stretch bent to detach the pistol from Thane's trembling hand and passed it to one of the lawmen now lurching to their feet.

"His timin' was bad," he drawled, as he surrendered the weapon to the pallid Deputy Prince. "When he jerked the trigger, the doggone muzzle was pushin' against him."

"Here's your hogleg, Moss," Larry offered curtly. "You weren't about to use it, so I had to."

Warren Kipp now came stumbling up the steps.

"Miss Phoebe . . . ?" he asked anxiously.

"Kindly assist me to rise," muttered Blake. "And then, Mister Kipp, you'll oblige me by reviving my daughter, helping her to my surrey and taking her home." Stretch stepped across to help him to his feet. He frowned at the taller Texan, nodded his thanks and called an order to the bug-eyed Moss. "Sheriff, have Deputy Prince return the prisoners to the county jail. You'll then accompany me to the bakery."

While Warren urgently beckoned the approaching Doc Corkhill and dropped to his knees beside Phoebe, the judge watched Prince hustle the prisoners down to the waiting wagon. Milhauser had disappeared into the bakery with Dent at his heels.

"All right, Judge," nodded Moss. "Ready when you are."

"I'll take a look at this man first," Blake decided.

After a thoughtful scrutiny of the face of the dead man, he descenderd to the street to slowly follow Moss to the bakery. The scene that confronted them caused Moss to curse explosively.

"Some mess, huh Orin?" remarked Dent.

Perched on a stool beside his oven, one hand held to his aching face, the baker answered Milhauser's questions.

"Well, damnit, what happened anyway?" blustered Moss.

"It's not clear to you yet?" Dent asked caustically. "An attempt on the judge's life."

"There can be no doubt about that," muttered Blake. "The bullet came within inches, actually bored into the wall between us."

"Bad shock for Phoebe," frowned Dent. "And for you, of course."

Blake stared hard at the body draped over the table.

"We'll go to the jail now, Sheriff," he said quietly. "I can identify both men. And I find myself in the embarrassing position of owing my life to two men on whom I passed sentence today."

Back in the double cell, the Texans lounged on their bunks and fixed jaundiced eyes on the irate, acutely humiliated Jesse Prince. Stretch yawned boredly, fished out a kerchief and dabbed at the scratches inflicted by the kill-crazy Thane.

"You think this'll win you any

privileges — you two smart-aleck show-offs?" cried Prince. "Tryin' to make me and Cleaver look foolish, huh? Playin' hero . . . !"

"I could sure admire your mouth, Prince," drawled Larry, "if you kept it shut."

"By Judas, you'll rue this day!" raged Prince, whirling to hurry along the passage. Reaching the connecting doorway, he turned again to yell taunts. "Four more days you'll be stuck here — and I promise you — they'll be four days of misery for you sonsabitches! You eat swill! And I'll find chores for you!" Unaware of the men entering from the street, he began yelling louder. "I'll have you cleanin' the cess-pool in the jailhouse yards — every day — so how d'you like *that*? Dirty chores, nothin' but swill to eat — I'm gonna give you hell, hear . . . ?"

"Jesse!" Moss said sharply.

"By the time we turn you loose from this jail," vowed Prince, "you'll be near starved — and you'll *stink* . . . !"

"*Shuddup*, Jesse, consarn you!" gasped Moss.

At Moss' second reprimand, Prince turned to gape. The sheriff wasn't alone. With him were Judge Blake, Roy Dent and Doc Corkhill, the latter with his little valise in the crook of his arm. They were studying Prince intently, their expressions eloquent. First to speak, Blake said coldly,

"Of course you'd never make good on those threats, Prince."

With a bleak smile, Dent challenged,

"You don't really mean a word of it, do you? You're just a little excited?"

"Jesse, you better not say nothin'," mumbled Moss. "Not one word." He unhitched his keyring. "We'll go in now, Judge."

Moments later, the double-cell had three extra occupants. While Moss hovered in the passage, angrily calling to Updike to cease his pleas for liquor, Doc squatted beside Stretch, opened his bag and began applying iodine to his scratched cheeks. Dent chose to remain standing and, when Larry offered his bunk to the judge, the newspaperman assured him,

"The judge would prefer to stay on his feet."

"I appreciate the offer, Mister Valentine," said Blake. "In my condition, rising from that bunk would be quite a chore for me. And painful, even with yours and Roy's help."

"I've been shot at and near killed!" Updike wailed from along the passage. "My nerves're jumpin', so I need a drink! You tell him, Doc! For medicinal purposes?"

"Let up on that caterwaulin', Updike!" roared Moss.

"You needn't wait there, Sheriff," said Blake, without shifting his gaze from the Texans. "We'll call you when we're ready to leave." After Moss had returned to the office, he delivered his short speech. "For the first time, I am indebted to men on whom I have passed sentence. Please accept my gratitude. Had either of those assassins succeeded . . . ”

“Forget it,” shrugged Larry. “You don't have to feel beholden.”

“It's hardly likely I'll forget, believe me,” countered Blake. “Mine wasn't the only life in danger.”

“Miss Phoebe was right by her father's side, Valentine,” Dent pointed out.

“Spirits of ammonia will do it every time,” muttered Doc. “She'll be home by now, Orin, pulling herself together and probably fixing coffee for young Kipp.”

“I can't show favoritism — as I'm sure you realize,” Blake told Larry.

“You got no call to apologize to the likes of us, Judge,” shrugged Stretch. “What's four days?”

“There were a whole heap of charges against us,” said Larry. “Four days for bustin' Rober's window seems fair enough.”

“I'm embarrassed even so,” said Blake.

"Maybe," nodded Larry. "But you don't have to be."

"I can't order your release," said Blake. "However, this much I assure you. Deputy Prince won't dare fulfill his wild threats. You won't be cleaning cess-pools."

"Nor eatin' swill?" Stretch asked hopefully.

Blake and Dent traded grins.

"On the contrary," said Blake. "If I know my daughter, you can look forward to better than jailhouse fare. It wouldn't surprise me if Phoebe cooked and served your meals in person."

"Wouldn't surprise me either," said Dent.

"Nor me," grunted Doc, rising to study his handiwork. "Well, my way-up-there friend, your face has probably looked better, but you don't seem the conceited type. What matters is there'll be no infection. And those scratches will heal."

"And then I'll be purty again," quipped Stretch.

"We'd best leave now," Blake suggested.

Dent retreated to the cell-door to summon the sheriff, then eyed Larry expectantly.

"Not curious, Valentine?" he challenged.

"About what?" asked Larry.

"My friend the judge has identified his would-be assassins," said Dent. "Both escapees from Bormann. The man your partner put down was Miles Thane. You accounted for the sharpshooter in the bakery. Another runaway — name of Falstead."

Moss came trudging in to unlock the door. As his visitors began filing out, Larry announced,

"I got somethin' to tell the sheriff. Like you gents to hear it."

They moved into the passage and, after Moss relocked the door, waited patiently.

"Yeah, what?" growled Moss.

"My wallet's in your safe," Larry reminded him. "A hundred and . . ."

"Hundred and fifty," nodded Moss. "You saw me count it. And I wrote you a regular receipt. So . . . ?"

"Take fifty out," instructed Larry. "It's for young Warren. He didn't ask for a — what d'you call it . . . ?"

"A retainer?" suggested Dent.

"That's it," said Larry. "He hasn't yet collected a dime for defendin' us."

"And he did real good," remarked Stretch. "Clumsy he is, but not 'tween his ears."

"Pay Warren the fifty," Larry told Moss.

"You'll see to that of course, Sheriff Moss?" frowned Blake.

"Certainly, Judge," shrugged Moss. "Take care of it rightaway."

Left alone, the Texans flopped on their bunks and traded thoughtful glances.

"You ain't forgettin' our three hundred that Rober cheated you of," guessed Stretch. "But you got somethin' else on your mind now, huh? If two of them jailbreakers that hates the judge's guts could dodge the huntin' parties and . . . "

"And make it to Alvison," muttered Larry. "And do their damnedest to kill Judge Blake."

"Uh huh," grunted Stretch. "If two of 'em could make it to Alvison, the others maybe could. All three of 'em."

"There'll be bulletins — with pictures — and we'll be out of this calaboose in four days," said Larry. "Might be it's time I asked Dutch to do me a favor."

"Like, for instance, sneakin' them handbills into us," suggested Stretch, "so we'll know them killers — if we do run into 'em?"

"You readin' my mind," nodded Larry.

Beyond the county jail, before parting company with the judge, Roy Dent reminded him,

"Right when your lives were in danger, yours and Phoebe's, it wasn't our sheriff or his cousin who rushed to your defense."

"Sad but true, Roy," sighed Blake.

"It had to be a couple of footloose outlaw-fighters — obeying their natural instincts," said Dent. "Something else you should know, Orin. Phin and I were uptown some distance, talking to Dutch Milhauser, when we heard the first shot. You must be aware of the prevailing attitude toward Dutch — since the Settlers Trust affair?"

"Well aware," nodded Blake.

"While that first shot was still echoing, Dutch drew his Colt and got moving — straight for Holmark's Bakery," Dent told him. "If Valentine's bullet had missed, I'm certain Dutch would have barged in there to do his duty. Other people saw him, people who've treated him with contempt this past year. Something to think about, isn't it?"

"Something I *will* think about," Blake assured him.

While the judge made his way homeward, another Bormann runaway was cocking a rifle some distance to the northeast of Alvison County. Cole Alton, Carl Craig, Gus Pinchon and Wolf Martell were heavily masked and staked out in rocks beside a bend of the stage-route to the Logan Spring switch station, an overnight stop for southbound coaches of the Gravitt & Sims Line.

"I'll take care of the guard," Alton said coolly, as he lined his sights. "useful target practice, you know? We'll call this a rehearsal for a more important killing. The shotgun-guard now and — in the near future — His Honor Judge Orin Blake."

6

Killer Number 3

THE bark of the rifle was followed by Craig's bellowed command. With a shocked oath, the driver hauled back on his reins. The shotgun was clattering to the ground, the guard about to topple, blood welling from his mortal wound. Hastily applying the brake, the driver grabbed at him.

"Bushwhackers!" he raged. "Lousy — yeller-bellied — bushwhackers . . . !"

The guard died in the driver's arms and was shoved back to flop against the baggage lashed to the roof. Inside the stalled vehicle, a woman screamed.

"Everybody out!" Craig repeated. "Climb on out with your hands up!"

"Any hero shows a gun, he just *knows*

what'll happen to him," chuckled Pinchon.

There were no heroes, just three men of advanced years and two terrified women, one of whom fainted and collapsed after descending to the trail. Wild-eyed, the driver glowered at the ambushers. If he held any hope of memorizing details of their appearance, offering descriptions to the Billingsville sheriff, that hope was at once dashed. They were hooded. Dusters and slickers shrouded them.

"The cashbox — throw it down," growled Craig.

"Here's the key that goes with it," jibed the driver. He tossed the key after dislodging the strongbox and letting it drop. "For all it'll profit you to open the box. We're carryin' no cash, just mail. That's all my partner's life was worth?"

Alton stayed mounted, his rifle covering the driver, while his cohorts swung down, Craig to check the contents of the strongbox, Pinchon and Martell to relieve the passengers of their cash. Watches and jewelry were ignored. They were after cash only. Having unlocked and opened the strongbox, he checked the contents and sourly remarked to Alton,

"Just mail."

Having pocketed the cash taken from the passengers, Pinchon and Martell returned to their horses. The half-breed, last to raise boot to stirrup, paused to heed Alton's command.

"Better for us if they're slowed down. The harness. You have a knife. Use it."

As he advanced on the team, Martell drew a knife. The driver began to protest, but was silenced by Craig.

"You got too big a mouth. Open it again and I'll aim a bullet at it."

Chuckling, Martell sliced at sections of the harness. Then, enjoying the revulsion of the one conscious female traveler, he slashed at the neck of the leftside team leader. The butchered animal flopped grotesquely and, clasping a hand to her mouth, the woman stumbled to the side of the trail to be sick. Martell's high-pitched laughter started scalps crawling.

"How about one of them?" he suggested, gesturing to the male passengers with his dripping blade.

"Get mounted," ordered Alton. "Let's waste no more time here."

The four were a good distance south of that bend, spelling their animals in a cedar grove, before Craig tallied the results of their treacherous labors.

"Scarce four hundred, Cole," he complained. "My friends and I have expensive tastes. You got to do better for us."

They hunkered beside their horses minus hoods and dusters, smoking, taking turns to swig from a bottle. Alton's counter to Craig's complaint was off-hand.

"You wanted to hit a stage because you were feeling lucky. I agreed to go along with it, but I warned you we could end up with nickels and dimes, remember?"

"Something *you* should remember," muttered Craig. "We have a deal."

"Ain't forgettin' we busted you out of Bormann, are you?" challenged Pinchon. "We took a chance, Alton, and not just because we like your looks. You promised Carl somethin'."

"I don't go back on my word," Alton said curtly.

"The Gilford Reliance Bank in Laramie," said Craig. "For five months I was working for that outfit as cashier. Five whole months, Cole."

"Until you tired of honest work," grinned Alton.

"Until I learned the combination to the vault," growled Craig. "This'll be the biggest job any of us ever pulled, but three men aren't enough. We need you, and that's why I went looking for Wolf and set up the breakout — just the way you ordered. So now you're out and free, and you owe me."

"Laramie's thataway," drawled Pinchon, jerking a thumb.

"And Alvison's in that direction,"

said Alton. He imitated Pinchon's action and bluntly assured Craig, "I'll side you on that Laramie deal, but you've waited quite a time, haven't you? What difference will another week make? Seven days. Maybe not that long." His eyes narrowed. A nerve twitched at his cheekbone. "I need to take care of Blake. You know that. It's what I've dreamed of all the years I was stuck in Bormann. He sent me there. I swore I'd settle with him for that — and nothing's gonna stop me."

"You'll be no use to us till you get that damn judge out of your system," Craig said resignedly.

"So what's to argue about?" shrugged Alton. "The deal still stands. You back my play in Alvison and, from there, we'll be Laramie-bound."

"I guess that's how it's got to be, Carl," said Pinchon.

"All right," nodded Craig. "First Alvison — then Laramie."

* * *

Five o'clock that afternoon, Warren Kipp appeared in the jailhouse passage. Milhauser had smuggled three handbills to the Texans a short time before. They now stashed those official bulletins under a blanket and eyed the young lawyer in polite enquiry.

"Sheriff Moss has paid me on your behalf," he gravely informed Larry. "So much, Mister Valentine! I assure you — I would never have demanded so high a fee. Are you sure you can afford . . . ?"

"Quit your frettin', boy," chided Stretch.

"You earned it," Larry insisted. "Did your damnedest for us."

"Mister Dent is more to be thanked than I," sighed Warren. "Of course Doctor Corkhill was an excellent witness. But, as you must have observed, I don't make a big impression. Not the way Mister Edmunds does. Nor Ross Gregory."

"Don't spend all of that fifty in one place," Larry good-humoredly advised.

"Well, a great deal of it will go to Mayor Grove from whom I rent my office and living quarters," said Warren. "I'm not earning much from my practice, I regret to say, and have fallen behind in my payments to the mayor. Also, I have purchased a pistol — second-hand — which cost me twelve dollars and twenty-five cents."

"Howzat again?" blinked Stretch.

"You've done *what*?" challenged Larry, studying him dubiously.

"I believe the weapon will be quite satisfactory to my purpose," said Warren. "I can't show it to you. Naturally, I had to leave it with Deputy Milhauser before coming in here."

"Satisfactory to your purpose?" prodded Larry.

"To be used only as an emergency," Warren explained. "I felt so — inadequate — during those attempts on Judge Blake's life. And Miss Phoebe's danger was just as great. I'm not a heroic person, gentlemen, but my concern for the judge's welfare — and for Miss Phoebe's — demands that I be ready to offer them my protection should the need arise."

"That's a chore for the law," warned Larry.

"Two escaped murderers, men who swore to avenge themselves, tried to kill the judge today," Warren reminded him. "The law, as I understand it, was found wanting. Had you gentlemen not intervened — at great risk to your own lives . . . "

"We just happened to be there is all," Larry said impatiently. "And we savvy guns, which you likely don't."

"No offense, son," drawled Stretch. "But, to me, you don't look like Sure-Shot Kipp, the fastest draw in the West."

"Should it be necessary, I'm sure I'll manage," said Warren. He nodded solemnly before leaving. "Thank you again for your prompt and generous payment for my services."

When Milhauser re-entered the

cellblock, the tall men were through studying the bulletins and committing three faces to memory. They ambled to the bars to return the papers. As the deputy stowed them inside his shirt, Larry addressed him worriedly.

"Dammit, Dutch, that puny lawyer-boy got himself a hogleg."

"Yeah," nodded Milhauser. "Bought it from a gunsmith name of Studlow. I know Matt Studlow pretty good. He wouldn't sell young Warren a faulty pistol."

"If that young'un tries to stash a Remington Army or a regular Colt in his belt, it'll drag his pants off," fretted Stretch.

"I wouldn't worry," shrugged Milhauser. "While he was talkin' to you, I checked it over."

"What kind of iron?" demanded Larry.

"Smith and Wesson thirty-eight," said Milhauser. "He'll likely tote it in a pocket."

"That fool boy wanderin' around

with a pocketful of Smith and Wesson," scowled Larry.

"Double action model," said Milhauser. "Barrel's cut way down." He propped a shoulder against the bars, showed Larry a rueful, slightly reproachful grin. "Valentine, you beat my time today."

"Is that so?" prodded Larry.

"Sharpshooter in the bakery," muttered the deputy. "I spotted the rifle-muzzle right after the shot, started down there fast. My chance to nail a killer, maybe take him alive, but you beat me to it. Tell me something'. Whose gun did you use?"

"Moss'," said Larry.

"They looked kind of pitiful, I guess, just a'lyin' there," drawled Stretch.

"Flat on their faces, Moss and Prince," Larry said in disgust. "Guns in their hands and too spooked to even cock 'em."

"Likely sounds far-fetched," frowned Milhauser. "The other three showin' up, I mean. Billy Bob or Melville or Alton. Mister Dent'll run a story about Thane and Falstead and maybe the news'll reach'em. They'll decide Alvison's too hot for 'em."

"Or, if they're all that kill-crazy," countered Larry, "they just might try it anyway."

"All that hate," reflected Milhauser. "All that hungerin' for vengeance could twist a man's brain. So maybe they'd be crazy enough." He straightened up and patted his shirt. "I'd best sneak these dodgers back into the files."

"Gonna take another look at them runaways' faces, Dutch?" asked Stretch.

"Don't need to," Milhauser said gruffly, raising a finger to his temple. "I got'em good and clear in my memory-box, by damn. Any of 'em shows, I'll know him for sure."

"If you see him first," said Larry.

"What the hell?" shrugged Milhauser. "My luck has to get better. Couldn't get much worse. 'Be seein' you."

At suppertime, Jug Updike was one envious prisoner. The coming

175

of Phoebe Blake caused a flurry of excitement in the sheriff's office. Prince mumbled something unintelligible when the judge's smiling daughter entered with a laden, cloth-covered tray and cheerily announced,

"For two gallant Texas gentlemen, supper is served."

"Glad to see you up and about again, Miss Phoebe," frowned Moss.

"Sheriff, I wasn't taken ill," she shrugged. "And, thanks to Doctor Corkhill, my fainting fit lasted only a little while. Well? Do I go right in, or do you wish to inspect the food? Chicken salad, apple pie and cream, two jugs of coffee."

"You can go right in," muttered Moss.

As well as ushering the visitor into the jailhouse, he carried a chair in for her. Resentment seethed within him, but he dared not show it. Somehow, he would have to regain favor with Judge Blake. Not only was Blake a close friend of the editor of the Sentinel; he was just as close to Mayor Chester Grove. And too many locals had witnessed his and Prince's poor performance this afternoon.

For the trouble-shooters, this was a far better than average supper, especially as their visitor chose to seat herself by their cell door and socialize with them.

"You can't eat and talk at the same time," she pointed out, as they began paying her cuisine the ultimate compliment.

"Well, shucks no," mumbled Stretch, after swallowing his first mouthful. "That wouldn't be polite."

"So I'll talk," she offered.

"You do that, Miss Phoebe," urged Larry, flashing her an appreciative grin. "Any lady can dish up such elegant chicken, she can bend my ear any time."

"I like to keep busy," she explained. "So, really, it'll be no trouble at all."

"That's fine," nodded Larry, raising a forkful of chicken, tomato and pickle.

"And just what'll be no trouble?"

"Keeping you well-fed till you're released," she smiled. "You're going to enjoy your breakfast, I'm sure. How does ham, eggs and hot biscuits sound? And, for tomorrow's lunch, I'm planning . . . "

"Um — uh — listen now, little lady." Larry munched, swallowed and addressed her very seriously. "What we did, it just came natural to us."

"Wasn't nothin'," Stretch assured her.

"Your pa already thanked us," said Larry. "I told him he don't owe us and that's what I'm tellin' you. No call for you to fetch all this fine chow all the time."

"Miser Valentine, if I tried to put my gratitude into words, I'm sure I'd be tongue-tied," she murmured. "So this is my way, a very small way, of expressing my feelings. And now . . . " She was smiling again. "Let's not be so serious. I want to tell you how much I enjoyed your trial. And, when Dad

178

sentenced you to only four days, I was delighted!"

"It sounded good to us too," remarked Stretch. "We was figurin' thirty days maybe."

"Young Warren did just fine," declared Larry.

"I think he showed more confidence today," said Phoebe. "Heaven knows the poor man *needs* confidence. He's so unsure of himself. When he calls on me, he seems lost for conversations. I have to keep leading him, trying to draw him out."

"You want to talk about Warren, that's okay by us," offered Larry. "We're kind of partial to him too."

From his cell, while trying to digest a less appetizing supper, the town drunk called pleadingly to the visitor

"Hey, ma'am, you fetch any booze?"

"Be quiet, Mister Updike," chided Phoebe.

"How about rope?" asked Updike. "You got any rope?"

"Of course not," she replied. "Why

179

ask such a foolish question?"

"If I don't soon taste some booze, I'm gonna hang myself," explained Updike. "For that, I need rope."

Winking at Phoebe, Larry called advice.

"Use your belt."

"And get found dead with my pants down?" retorted Updike. "Doggone it, I got my standards."

After her giggles subsided, Phoebe made him an offer.

"Mister Updike, if you'll promise to stop complaining, there'll be an extra plate on the breakfast tray for you."

And so, to the chagrin of Sheriff Moss and his cousin, Phoebe Blake's visits continued over the next few days. No other suspicious characters were sighted during that period, no gun-toting strangers were seen loitering in the vicinity of the Blake home.

But trouble was on the way, mounted, armed and respectably attired.

Keeping up appearances had always been one of Vernon Melville's strong points. His luck changed for the better when, with ridiculous ease, he equipped himself for his journey to Alvison at the expense of a prosperous cattleman whose sprawling ranch was located to the north.

It seemed everything was going Melville's way. He reached the Bar 9 spread of Carney County 10 o'clock of the night of a big celebration, the festivities following the marriage of the rancher's only daughter. The guests were entertained in the broad yard fronting the ranch-house, dining on barbecued beef in bright lamplight and drinking their fill at the bar set up by their host. The house, Melville found, was almost deserted.

By climbing a tree, he reached the roof and made a tricky descent to an open window. And his luck was holding; he had found the master bedroom. Better than that, he was of similar build to the master of Bar 9.

When Melville made his way to a barn to help himself to a horse and

181

saddle, he was toting his prison garb and wearing a suit of expensive grey broadcloth, checkered vest, tasteful shirt and cravat and a fine new derby. The rancher's handsome gunbelt girded his loins, the butt of an ebony-gripped Colt jutting from the holster. In his pockets, he toted scissors, a razor and $250 he had found in a dresser drawer.

Two miles south of Bar 9 range, with nobody the wiser, Melville tethered his stolen horse and spelled the animal during the time it took to bury his prison outfit. Next morning at a mountain spring, he bathed, trimmed his hair and rid himself of his beard. By the time he re-donned his finery, he was clean-shaven except for a neatly-clipped mustache, an impressive six-footer, audacious, presentable, ingratiating — and grimly determined to spill the blood of the man he hated.

Early afternoon of the day before the Texans' release from the county jail, Melville rode into Alvison and made straight for the headquarters of an old cohort. When he entered the Palace of Joy, off-duty Deputy Milhauser was seated behind a tall beer at a table left of the entrance. At once he began sizing up the newcomer, comparing his features with one of three photographs. And at once Melville glanced his way, noted the badge on the vest and took the initiative.

"'Afternoon, Deputy." He nodded affably. "Hartley's the name, Emmett Hartley, here for a little reunion with an old friend. Neeley Rober around?"

"Went up to his office just a couple minutes ago," offered Milhauser, nodding to the stairs.

Melville thanked him with a broad grin and strode briskly to the stairs while Milhauser decided,

'My mistake. No Bormann runaway would have the nerve to brace a lawman like that.'

Confronted by the well-groomed escapee, Rober rose from behind his desk and gaped incredulously.

"Neeler," nodded Melville.

"You haven't changed a bit."

"Hell's fire!" breathed Rober. "I can't say the same of you. Damn it, Vern, if it wasn't for your voice . . . "

"Clothes make the man," shrugged Melville, perched on the edge of the desk. "And a razor helps. Well no, you can guess why I'm here."

At his liquor cabinet now, pouring generous shots of his best bourbon, Rober grinned an ugly grin.

"Sure, Vern. I can guess."

"Outside of that drink, there's only one thing I'm asking of you — for old times sake," drawled Melville.

"Way ahead of you, old pal, way ahead of you," chuckled Rober.

While they disposed of the bourbon, he offered Melville directions to the Blake home on Mailey Street. The house was described, the whole domestic set-up, and Melville was well satisfied.

"Obliged to you, Neeley." He drained his glass. "So now I get it done. One shot is all it's going to take, and then I'll be Idaho-bound."

"Means a lot to you, huh?" prodded Rober. "Putting him down?"

"His face has been in my dreams," muttered Melville. "Him with his oh-so-solemn look — solemn and sorrowful — as though he didn't enjoy sending me away for life. Only one way I'll rid my mind of that dream, Neeley. I have to see him fall before my gun. I'll enjoy killing him — as much as he enjoys being a self-righteous hypocrite." The spasm of emotion quickly passed. He set his empty glass down and nodded genially. "Thanks for the cheer, friend."

"All the luck, Vern," Rober said fervently.

Some ten minutes later, when Melville sounded the doorbell at the Blake house, Phoebe was entertaining a gentleman-friend in the parlor off the front hall. Warren Kipp was paying her yet another tongue-tied visit and, as was his wont, her father had discreetly excused himself and retreated to his study.

As she rose to quit the parlor, Phoebe showed her guest a reassuring smile.

"It's probably Ross, but you shouldn't mind. Don't be so *timid*, Warren. Relax. He doesn't dislike you and you don't dislike him."

That reassuring smile had done nothing for the young lawyer. He was out of his chair and pacing restlessly, cocking an ear, when Phoebe opened the front door to trade smiles and greetings with a courteous stranger.

"Miss Blake, I presume?" Melville bared his head and accorded her a bow. "Emmett Hartley — representing the Preston company, a new publishing house specializing in law books. I have traveled a considerable distance, so I trust I'll not be disappointed. Your father, Judge Orin Blake, is at home?"

"Dad has *so many* books, Mister Hartley," warned Phoebe. "But come in by all means. If you'll wait a few moments, I'll tell him you're here."

To Warren's disquiet, the strange voice started his scalp crawling. He moved to the parlor entrance to trade nods with Melville, his hands thrust in his coat pockets. To his further disquiet, he instinctively gripped the pistol in the right pocket.

"Dad, a Mister Hartley," called Phoebe. "From the Preston book company?"

The reply, that well-remembered voice, shattered Melville's poise.

"Ask the gentleman to wait. And you may bring me his credentials."

Melville's animal-like growl caused Pheobe to whirl and stare at him. He had emptied his holster. The muzzle of a Colt .45 was directed at her head.

"Come out and face me, Judge Blake!" he ordered. "My gun's on your precious daughter! She's dead if you aren't out of there by the time I count to three!" he bared his teeth. One . . . !"

"Wait — *no* . . . !" gasped Warren.

He took a step forward and, automatically, Melville swung the Colt to cover him. Menaced by that cocked weapon, he recoiled in horror, lost his footing and began falling, and his index finger was curled around the Smith & Wesson's trigger. The weapon discharged as he went down and Phoebe, shocked by the sudden bloody condition of Melville's chest, loosed a scream of anguish. Face contorted, Melville reeled and slumped against the rightside wall. He raised his left hand to his chest and cursed luridly. In his sagging right hand, the Colt roared thunderously. The bullet tore Warren's pants-leg before embedding in the floor. And then, while Warren struggled to extricate hand and pistol from his smoldering pocket, Melville's curses ceased. He went down heavily to die in an awkward, seated posture.

"Dad — it's all right!" cried Phoebe. "I'm not hurt! But — poor, dear Warren . . . !"

Pallid and trembling, Blake emerged from the study to work himself into the hall and study that grim scene. He winced and, balancing on his crutches, stared from the dead man to Warren and his daughter.

The young lawyer was lurching upright and mumbling to Phoebe to stay clear of him. Not only had the .38 slug bored a hole through his pocket. The flash of the discharge had ignited the material, and now the air was invaded by pungent-smelling smoke.

"Please, Phoebe! I can — manage . . . !"

Despairing of extricating the pistol, Warren peeled off his coat and shook it. The Smith & Wesson thudded to the floor. He then dropped the coat and stamped on it until the smoldering subsided.

"Oh, Dad, he was so brave!" gasped Phoebe. "And — this time — I won't faint — I promise!"

Fists pounded at the front door. Blake, bending to study the dead man, urged Phoebe to open up.

"Whoever it is, tell them to send for the sheriff."

A few minutes later, when Cleaver

Moss barged through the muttering neighbors on the front porch, Blake was still hovering by the body of his would-be assassin. Warren had retreated into the parlor with Phoebe after retrieving his pistol, applying the safety catch and stowing it in his hip pocket. He was seated now with Phoebe fussing over him, his face haggard, his stunned gaze on his torn pants-leg.

"Hell's bells!" gasped Moss.

"You'll oblige me by having the body removed to the funeral parlor," muttered Blake.

"Dammit, Judge, what . . . ?" began Moss.

"He gained entry by posing as a book salesman," said Blake. "I can identify him. As I recall, he was clean-shaven when I sentenced him to Bormann for life. He's older now, of course, but I'm sure of him."

"You sayin' he — uh — he's another of them jailbreakers?" challenged Moss.

"Vernon Melville."

"And — you shot him?"

"Warren Kipp shot him."

"*Kipp . . . ?*"

"Accidentally I believe. My daughter saw the whole thing. You may question her, Sheriff. But gently — patiently. Is that understood?"

"Well, sure, Judge," frowned Moss. "Understood."

Within the quarter-hour, the body had been removed and statements taken from Phoebe and her badly-shaken admirer, who were then called into her father's study. Blake had filled three glasses from a brandy bottle.

"Badly needed, I think," he said, as they seated themselves. "Go ahead my child. You too, Warren. You're both pale as death." He took a pull at his own drink and shook his head sadly. "Phoebe, I spoke without thinking. When I asked you to bring me the man's credentials — I provoked him — put your life in jeopardy."

"You couldn't have foreseen," she consoled him.

She sipped her brandy and he saw

the color return to her cheeks. Warren gulped a mouthful, coughed and bowed his head. He could think of nothing to say, but Blake could.

"Not very long ago, I had to thank those Texans for saving my life — and probably my daughter's," he told Warren. "And now it's you I must thank."

"No credit to me, sir," sighed Warren. "I've no talent for such — activity. My pistol was accidentally discharged, though I pulled the trigger. It was a reflex action — when I fell — terrified that man would shoot me."

"At least there's a practical way I can show my gratitude," said Blake. "If you'll pardon my asking, was that your only suit?" Warren nodded uncomfortably. "Tomorrow morning, come by for me and take me to Byrd's tailor shop. I'm going to have Max Byrd measure you for a new suit. In the cloth of your choice, of course."

"But — Mister Byrd is the most

expensive tailor in town!" Warren protested.

"Call it a gift," smiled Blake. "A small gesture of appreciation. Let's make it early. Nine-thirty?"

Having followed Carbro's rig to the funeral parlor and viewed the body, Deputy Milhauser was fired with the urge to dash to the Palace of Joy and confront Rober. He headed in that direction and was actually in sight of the saloon when he glimpsed the sheriff disappearing through the entrance. Halting in his tracks, he fished out his makings to roll a cigarette.

'No use,' he decided. 'Not while he's with Moss. Partners they are, and close. I try accusin' Rober of anything, Moss'll stand by him, likely threaten to have me fired. Some eagle-eyed lawman I am. Never forget a face. Oh, sure. That bastard Melville. I should've recognized him — and I didn't.'

Who to turn to now? He made his decision, lit his cigarette and began ambling toward the law office, while

Moss and Rober held council in the office at the Palace of Joy.

The sheriff's hands trembled as he poured himself a shot of whiskey.

"That makes three out of five!" he complained. "Hell, Neeley, as if it wasn't bad enough the trouble-shooters downed them first two. Now that chicken-livered Lawyer-boy's made himself a hero!"

"You and Jesse are looking bad, and that's trouble," Rober agreed. "But that's not the half of it, Cleaver. We've got *worse* trouble."

7

Killer Number 4

ROY DENT, as Rober now reminded the sheriff, had reported the trial of Valentine and Emerson in considerable detail, emphasizing vital aspects of both prosecution and defense testimony. That edition had been a sell-out, Dent having made space for a report on the attempt on Judge Blake's life and the deaths of Thane and Falstead.

"So Valentine's suddenly a hero and winning sympathy," complained Rober. "And that's affecting our business."

"Your sure of this?" frowned Moss.

"Why wouldn't I be sure?" challenged Rober. "You want to check our books? Townmen have been staying clear of the gambling tables these past few days. So our profits are down."

"Tomorrow the ranch-hands'll be in town and we'll do better," opined Moss. "Pay-day for all the spreads hereabouts."

"You think cowhands can't read?" scowled Rober. "They'll be as leery as the townmen."

"Maybe not," argued Moss. "I'm bettin' Roy Dent'll put out a special edition. He won't miss a chance to make an extra buck out of this Melville thing. And that'll give our customers somethin' else to think about."

"The suckers aren't forgetting Valentine's accusations against me," fretted Rober. "There's a lot of talk. Cleaver, a lot of bad feeling. We could be wiped out — especially if that special committee is formed."

Moss finished his drink, poured himself a refill and flopped into a chair to eye his partner in alarm.

"Special committee — for what?" he demanded. "How come I ain't heard of it?"

"So far, all I hear is a rumor,"

muttered Rober. "Something about a committee being formed to investigate all the gambling activity in Alvison, every saloon offering games of chance. The mayor has been petitioned, or so they say. It's being hinted at that he'll invite Judge Blake to become an honorary member of the committee." He cursed bitterly. "That's why I was so damn glad to see Melville. Blake's a popular figure. With him out of the way, and with the mayor coming up for re-election next month, we'd stand a better chance of surviving an investigation. I could maybe get to Chet Grove."

Moss' jaw sagged.

"You — saw Melville — that runaway?"

"Knew him from a long time back," shrugged Rober. "Don't worry about it. If anybody gets curious, I only have to say I knew him under another name and had no idea he was Vern Melville."

"Damn and blast," breathed Moss.

"Them proddy Texans — they're nothin' but trouble."

"I'll be counting on you and Jesse tomorrow," said Rober. "Your badge and Jesse's fancy gun are all it takes to keep the cowboys in line. If there's any kind of demonstration, you know what to do. Throw a few of them in jail and the rest will back off."

"You'd better be right about that," Moss said worriedly.

The moment he entered the office, Milhauser was challenged by Prince.

"It's true — what every big-mouth keeps stoppin' by to tell me? Another of them runaways, and he got into the judge's house?"

"Carbro's layin' him out now," nodded Milhauser. "It was Melville all right."

"Shot by that fool Kipp?" Prince seethed with frustration. "A two-bit kid lawyer scared of his own shadow? *He* got Melville?"

"Kipp got him with a lucky shot," sighed Milhasuer, trudging to the cellblock entrance. "It should've been me."

"You?" sneered Prince. "Like hell. Your nerve'd fail if you found yourself up against a killer like Melville."

Milhauser unlocked the jailhouse door and, before opening it, turned to frown at the younger deputy. This past year, he had taken many an insult from Prince and the sheriff — and others. Off-duty, he had become a recluse, withdrawn, keeping to himself, showing no reaction to the scorn of his fellow-citizens. But now, poker-faced, he put a question to one of his most scathing critics.

"Speakin' of nerve, how did *you* feel when Falstead opened fire from the bakehouse?"

Prince turned beetroot-red and clenched his fists.

"Mind how you talk to me!" he gasped. "Me and Cleaver, we flopped on that top step because we didn't know where the shot came from! That's what any lawman does!"

199

"The way I hear it, Valentine didn't need but a couple seconds to guess where the shot came from," Milhauser quietly retorted. "And he did somethin' about it — with the sheriff's gun." Staring hard at the irate Prince, he muttered a warning. "From here on, boy, *you* mind how *you* talk to *me*."

With that, he opened the door to let himself into the jailhouse. He butted his cigarette when he reached the door of the double cell, fished out his makings and began building another. The Texans came to the bars as he began talking.

"Don't count on Phoebe Blake fixin' supper tonight. I'm guessin' you'll have to settle for whatever I bring you."

"Miss Phoebe's feelin' poorly?" enquired Stretch.

"It ain't just the good chow, Dutch," drawled Larry. "We kind of admire the lady."

"Big trouble at the Blake house," Milhauser reported. "She wasn't hurt and the judge is okay, but I'm bettin' she's all shook up." He went on to recount all he had learned of the latest attempt on Blake's life and its violent aftermath. "How do you like that Kipp boy? Crazy accident, I'd reckon. But mighty unlucky for Melville. Seems he took that thirty-eight slug dead-centre."

"Hol-eee Hannah," breathed Stretch. "Weak-Knee Warren and his double action hogleg."

"He'll be more shook up than Phoebe," opined Larry.

"Ain't that the truth," agreed Stretch. "Runt, you thinkin' what I'm thinkin'?"

"Damn right," nodded Larry. "This is a helluva time for us to be sittin' on our butts in a calaboose. Out of here is where we ought to be — so we can keep an eye on Blake." He eyed Milhauser impatiently. "Any bulletins on the other two?"

"We've had no word," said Milhauser. "Far as anybody knows, Alton and Billy Bob are still on the loose. Listen now, Valentine, you'll be set free tomorrow mornin', but that don't mean free to take the law into your own hands. Moss and Cousin Jesse are totin' heavy chips on their shoulders. They hate your guts. And they'll be lookin' for an excuse — any excuse — to nail you again. Somethin' else you'd better remember. I don't want to lock horns with you — and *I'll* be lookin' out for Alton or Billy Bob, whichever shows first."

"*If* they show," countered Stretch.

"They just might," opined Larry. "At the start, nobody believed *any* of em'd come to Alvison, but this makes three of the five." He grimaced in disgust. "Them sonsabitches sure crave Blake's blood."

"They've had a lot of time for buildin' up their spite," remarked Milhauser, also showing disgust.

"You got our word, Dutch," offered Larry. "We ain't lookin' to tangle with you."

"But just supposin' now," said Stretch. "Just supposin' we spot one of them killers before you do. You think we could make believe we don't know him?"

"I don't reckon you could do that," Milhauser said resignedly. He lit his cigarette and frowned at them through the smoke-haze. "Somethin' else I have to tell you. Gonna be a lot of excited bucks hittin' town tomorrow. It's Saturday. First Saturday of the month. Pay-day for all the county cattle outfits. Those ranch-hands'll have money in their pockets and an itch to let off steam. Do I have to say it? You can't afford to get prodded into a ruckus by some likkered-up cowboy cravin' to prove he's tougher than you."

"Everything happens to us," grouched Stretch.

"If it ain't minehands or town rowdies that challenge you two, it's cowhands," Milhauser reminded them. "I know. I've read all the reports. So, when you're turned loose, tread wary."

"We'll do that," promised Larry.

"And what else is stickin' in your craw, Dutch?" He studied Milhauser shrewdly. "Seems to me you're lookin' plenty sore right now."

"Sore at myself," Milhauser confided. "Melville walked right into the Palace and asked me where he could find Rober. Just like that. I thought I recognized him but, when he talked right up to me that way, I figured it couldn't be him."

"He asked for Rober?" frowned Larry.

"Went on up to Rober's office," nodded Milhauser. "Yeah, that's somethin' to think about huh?"

"Somethin' to remember," Larry decided.

"I ain't apt to forget it," declared Milhauser. "But, for now, I ain't sayin' anything. Sometimes it pays to play a waitin' game." Grimly, he added, "I'm good at that."

★ ★ ★

Nine o'clock next morning, released from their cell after an unappetizing breakfast, the Texans followed Milhauser into the office. The safe was unlocked and their personal effects returned to them by the scowling Prince. While they retrieved and strapped on their sidearms, Moss growled threats and warnings, all of which they ignored.

Unhurriedly they moved out into the sunshine to begin a leisurely search for a restaurant, a small cafe, some hole-in-wall diner, any place they could compensate their interiors for that earlier, less than adequate breakfast.

By the time Moss and his deputies were out and about, they had found their way to the Keeble Cafe, a small establishment two blocks uptown. There, while accounting for bacon and eggs at a front window table, they were presently joined by the amiable Doc Corkhill.

As he came bustling in, the runty medico was eagerly welcomed by Stretch.

"Just coffee, Amos," he called to the proprietor. "I'll be over here with my friends." Settling into the third chair, he put his little valise down and surveyed them cheerily. "A pleasure to see you boys at large again. How's the wound, Larry?"

"Healin' good, Doc," nodded Larry. "I took the dressin' off last night. Listen, we want to thank you for talkin' up for us in court."

"Just doing my duty to the law," shrugged Doc, as Keeble set coffee before him. "Well now, Alvison is getting to be a dangerous town, huh? For Orin Blake anyway. I suppose you've heard there's been another attempt on his life?"

"And young Warren's a hero," grinned Stretch.

"Which probably comes as a sizeable surprise to young Warren," retorted Doc. He sipped his coffee, watched them fork up generous mouthfuls and reverted to his pet preoccupation. "Diet maybe a contributory factor, yes indeed,

206

but I've also been thinking about the climatic conditions prevailing in the vast region between the Red River and the Rio Grande."

"He means Texas," Stretch told Larry.

"I didn't think he meant Minnesota," grunted Larry.

From where he sat, he commanded a clear view of Main Street and the opposite sidewalk for almost the entire block. The store a few doors down from the building directly opposite the cafe was a tailor's workshop; he easily read the sign above the door. From the doorway, a shirtsleeved, balding individual, tailor Max Byrd himself, was raising a hand to welcome an old client and a new one. Judge Blake was working himself along on his crutches accompanied by a self-conscious Warren Kipp, self-conscious at showing himself in public minus coat and with a visible tear in one pants-leg. Tagging the judge and his young companion was Deputy Prince, playing

207

his role of alert gunslinger-lawman to the hilt, treading purposefully, thumbs hooked in shell-belt.

The rider coming slowly along Main from its south end was beyond Larry's line of vision and winning little attention from passers-by, a lean, youngish man with lank black hair dangling from under a battered hat, buck-toothed and broken-nosed, his eyes bulbous, his chin receding. Shabby though he was, the Colt lashed to his right thigh looked brand-new. And businesslike.

Upon sighting Blake, the rider eased his boots from stirrups, dropped to the ground and emptied his holster.

"Hey, Judge!" His yelled greeting was following by an inane snigger. At once, Prince recognized him, startled convulsively and panicked. Billy Bob Grebb ignored him. He could afford to ignore a lawman who turned tail and ran for the nearest alleymouth. "Yah, Judge, it's me!" As Blake froze, he thumbed back his hammer, sniggered again and drew a bead on him. "No life sentence for you, old man. Sentence of death!"

Townfolk were stumbling in their haste to vacate that section of the street and a party of a dozen ranch-hands advancing along Main from the north, when Moss came bustling onto the scene. He bellowed a demand that Grebb drop his gun and surrender, but took fright when Grebb pulled another Colt from inside his shirt and pointed it his way; the boss-lawman collided with two other fleeing locals in his frantic haste to reach safe cover.

"Don't look like you're gettin' much protection, Judge," chuckled Grebb. "So here's somethin' for you — for old times sake!"

Petrified until this moment, Warren began a vain attempt to dissuade the killer from his purpose. He sidestepped quickly to position himself in front of Blake, shielding him with his body as he groped for the pistol in his hip pocket.

"You can't do it!" he gasped. "You'd

have to be insane — to want to shoot the judge in cold blood — before so many witnesses . . . !"

He was still trying to tug the Smith & Wesson from his hip when Grebb filled the air with strident laughter and the roar of the Colt in his right fist. The impact of the bullet threw Warren against Blake with such force that he was shoved off-balance; both men began collapsing.

At Keeble's, Larry gasped an oath and quit his chair. The front window was open and he wasn't about to lose time making for the entrance. He clambered from the window and barged into the street to quickly survey the situation, Blake huddled on the sidewalk a short distance from the tailor shop doorway, the unconscious Warren sprawled atop him, the cowhands pausing a half-block north. The two-gun-toting stranger, he realised, just had to be the infamous Billy Bob.

"You hombres stay back!" he yelled to the ranch-hands.

Grebb, about to move closer to his intended victim, glanced sidelong toward Larry, bared his buck teeth and called a warning.

"Better cut and run while you're alive enough, tall man! I ain't particular how many heroes I put down!"

Larry stood with legs slightly spread, right hand hovering over holster.

"Give up on it, Grebb!" he urged.

"You ain't backin' off?" demanded Grebb.

"Not so you'd notice," growled Larry.

His Colt cleared leather as the killer whirled on him. It roared a split-second before Grebb's righthand gun discharged and, though he flinched from the fiery breath of Grebb's bullet fanning his face, he stood his ground and quickly re-cocked. Staggering drunkenly, Grebb dropped his righthand gun and swung the other up. That weapon was lined on Larry when Larry fired again. And that did it for Billy Bob Grebb. He lurched backward, arms flailing, legs buckling. A small dust-cloud puffed up as he crashed shoulders-first in the centre of Main Street.

Now the cowhands urged their horses forward, some cheering the grim-faced Larry, others indignantly voicing what seemed a fair question. Where the hell were the local lawmen when most needed?

Milhauser, off-duty and hastily toweling himself dry in a bath-house far uptown, was the only peace officer whose non-participation was justified. Moss and Prince were now emerging to control the fast-growing crowd converging on the scene, both indignantly chiding the ranch-hands.

"I needed a firin' point from where I could get a shot at Grebb!" asserted Moss. "Got a responsibility to the townfolk, damnit! Main Street's no place for a shootout!"

"My — my gun jammed . . . " lied Prince. "Yeah, that's a fact! Right when I had a clear bead on Grebb!"

As he emerged from the cafe with Doc trotting at his side, the taller Texan re-holstered his righthand Colt.

"Your friend had first chance at that demented desperado," frowned the little medico. "If he had failed, you'd have made your play."

In their short relationship, this was to be the first and last vehement declaration voiced by Stretch.

"Any gunslick kills Larry, he get his from me."

They hurried to where Larry and the tailor were helping Blake to his feet, sparing no glance for the people gathering about the lifeless Grebb. While Blake balanced on his retrieved crutches and waited as patiently as he was able, Doc hunkered by the hapless Warren and began a cursory examination of his wound. Dent then arrived, more anxious than curious, more concerned for Blake's welfare than the news value of the gunfight.

"Let me help you home, Orin," he begged.

"I'll be grateful," nodded Blake. "But not before Phin decides the boy's chances. By thunder, Roy, his only thought was to protect me."

"He was shielding the judge," offered Byrd. "I'll tell you, Mister Dent, I took young Kipp pretty much for granted till I saw what he did just now, but . . ."

"I know what you mean," frowned Dent. "Young Warren, through circumstances he could not foresee, is showing himself in his true colors."

"Prince and the sheriff too," scowled Byrd. "They turned tail and ran . . ."

"Howzat again?" Larry challenged him.

"I saw it," said the tailor. "They ran scared, both of them. Didn't dare stand up to that killer. And we rely on them for protection!"

"Phin . . ." began Blake.

"Bullet lodged in left shoulder — the fleshy part," announced Doc, rising. "If my tall friends will bring him to my place rightaway, I'll remove the bullet as quickly as possible — the quicker the better. And there should still be time to protect him from an infection. Ready when you are, boys, I'll lead the way."

"So now you know as much as Phin can tell you, Orin," muttered Dent. "Come on. I'll take you home now."

Fully-dressed, cursing himself for having missed this action, Milhauser reached that area in time to see the sheriff supervising the removal of Grebb's body. He turned as a hand touched his arm to find himself trading stares with Ross Gregory.

"Off duty, I presume, Deputy?" the lawyer asked with a mirthless grin. "You have a look of an extremely disappointed man."

"So I look the way I feel, Mister Gregory," growled Milhauser. "Sure, I'm off duty. And I was soakin' in a tub at Findlater's when this all happened."

"The homicidal career of Bill Bob Grebb — that unsavory psychopath — brought to a decisive end by a shiftless drifter," sighed Gregory, "While you, a lawman yearning to redeem himself in the eyes of his fellow-citizens, were otherwise engaged. Believe me, I know exactly how you feel. I too am suffering the ultimate frustration and disappointment — my dream of marital bliss shattered."

"Mister Gregory, I don't know what you're talkin' about," frowned Milhauser.

"Of course you know," retorted Gregory. "All Alvison knows of my suit for the hand of the fair Phoebe, beloved and loyal daughter of our esteemed judge. I have *no* chance now, Deputy!"

"On account of Mister Kipp and what he did last night," guessed Milhauser.

"He's done it again!" complained Gregory. "This time more spectacularly and in broad daylight. Worse, he has suffered a wound while bravely striving to protect the judge. From this moment on, Phoebe will regard me as no more than a good friend. All her love and admiration will be concentrated on Warren — her hero." He grimaced in exasperation. "Confound it, I didn't want to be her friend. I wanted to be her husband. But now I've lost her."

"Yeah, well, I'm sorry," shrugged Milhauser.

"I intend getting drunk — right now," announced Gregory. "Be my guest, Emil. That's your first name, is it not? You're off-duty and miserable and so am I, so let's commiserate with each other over an endless succession of double-shots of good whiskey. Come! Let's Wassail at the Palace of Joy!"

"Wassail — what is that?" asked Milhauser, as they turned and made for the Palace. "Fancy word for wailin'? Well, I'm not about to wail and I don't reckon I'll get drunk, but I guess I'll side you a while, Mister Gregory, make sure you don't get disorderly as well as drunk. County jail's no place for a fine gentleman like you."

"Call me Ross," offered the lawyer.

Other hands from the county spreads were arriving and, by the time Milhauser and Gregory were seating themselves at a table near the bar, the Palace of Joy was filling up. Better than a score of thirsty cowpokes were discussing the shootout but, to the surprise of Rober's staff, quietly. Voices weren't raised. Many a grim glance was aimed at the portly proprietor. Rober moved among them, his welcoming grin a fixture, masking his apprehension.

After his first double-shot of bourbon, Gregory complained,

"That did nothing for me, Emil. Order refills. I'm buying."

"Hallo there, Counsellor!" Rober came to their table to effusively welcome the lawyer. "We don't see enough of you in the Palace." He switched his gaze to Milhauser and dubiously enquired, Are you two together?"

"What's the matter, Rober?" Milhauser raised his voice. As though that were a signal, the muttering of the ranch-hands

218

abated; curious frowns were aimed in their direction. "It seem strange to you — Mister Gregory and me drinkin' together?"

"Not strange," shrugged Rober. "Just — uh — a little unexpected, that's all."

"Like an escaped killer from Bormann walkin' in here yesterday and askin' for you," growled Milhauser. "Yeah, that was plenty unexpected. Turns out he was Vern Melville." As Rober's face reddened, he went on relentlessly. "Too bad I didn't recognizie him, Rober, But I guess you did — when he went up to your office to visit with you."

"This is interesting," remarked Gregory. "I mean, *really* interesting."

"Be damned careful, Deputy!" warned Rober. "There's a simple explanation. I had a slight acquaintance with the man I now know to have been Vernon Melville. When I knew him — years ago — he was calling himself Carson, and I was none the wiser." He too was raising his voice, appealing to his customers. "Of course I recognized Melville — but as Carson, when he walked into my office. He said he was working as a cattle-buyer nowadays, asked a few questions about the local ranchers and left. And, when I learned of what happened at Judge Blake's house, I was deeply shocked." He glowered at Milhauser. "Does that satisfy you, Deputy?"

Unflinchingly, Milhauser replied,

"Give me time. I'm still thinkin' on it."

Rober scowled angrily, turned and strode toward the stairs, but was jerked to a halt by the loud remark of a hefty ranch-hand.

"I don't know why we're drinkin' in this place. Why are we spendin' our coin in the Palace — after what we read in the newspaper?"

"Now, boys, you can't believe what you read . . . !" began Rober.

"We ain't so sure about that, Rober," growled another man. "The way we hear it, this Valentine jasper's no greenhorn when it comes to five card stud. If he claimed you was bottom-dealin' . . . "

"Valentine lied!" gasped Rober.

"So maybe *I'm* lyin'," challenged a veteran wrangler. "I've lost many a dollar on your games of chance, mister. And now I'm thinkin' maybe *I* got gypped, and wonderin' how many more of us been gypped at the Palace."

"Now see here!" protested Rober. "I don't have to stand for this!"

"What're you gonna do, Rober?" demanded the brawniest of his challengers. "Gonna turn Big Anse loose on us?" He flexed his muscles and studied the bouncer, the table supervisors, the barkeeps. "Big Anse and your other hired bully-boys? Try it, Rober. The way we're feelin', we'll make quite a fight of it — right, fellers?"

"Order refills, Emil," begged Gregory. "When this riot starts, I want to be drunk enough to enjoy it. I may even participate!"

"Forget it, Mister Gregory," chided Milhauser, as he began rising.

"Ross," corrected Gregory.

"Stay quiet, Ross," Milhauser advised.

"What're we waitin' for?" yelled an over-stimulated waddy. "Let's take this gyp-joint apart!"

"That's all, boys!" Milhauser called sharply. "Now listen up, all of you — in the name of law!" The county cowhands hadn't forgotten the Settlers' Trust affair. Maybe some of them looked on this deputy as a has-been, but as many others were eyeing him warily now. "You start raisin' hell in here, you know what I got to do. I can't lick you all, but this much I promise. Some of you will spend payday and Sunday in jail."

"Hey, Dutch, what d'you care if we give Rober a bad time?" another Waddy demanded. "You're no friend of his!"

"Hell, no," agreed Milhauser. "But I'm a lawman, son. I carry a badge and I do my duty the best way I can.

Now let's act reasonable. Plenty other saloons in town. There's good booze at the Glad Hand, at Morrison's, at the Pinto Stud. You don't like it here — why hang around? Do yourselves a favor, boys. Instead of raisin' hell, just move out quiet."

The payday gang had barely begun drinking, were not yet fired up to the point of defying the logic of the deputy's appeal. He won his point. They mumbled among themselves a few moments, then set their glasses down and began filing out.

When the last grim-faced waddy had left, Rober made for the stairs, calling to his staff en route.

"Don't stand for any rough stuff, boys. Be ready for anything."

It didn't occur to him, as he hurried upstairs, to pause and thank Milhauser for restoring order. Milhauser would have been surprised if he had.

"Come, Emil," urged Gregory. "As you so forcefully reminded those hotheads, there are other saloons.

The atmosphere of this place suddenly depresses me. So let's go elsewhere and wassail!"

"Thanks for the invite, Ross, but I'll tell you what," said Milhauser, helping him from his chair. "I don't reckon I ought to tie one on. Might be smarter for me to stay clear-eyed. And you don't want the whole town to see you stumblin' drunk, do you? So why don't you buy yourself a bottle, head home and do your wassailin' in private?"

Again, reason prevailed. The lawyer and the deputy parted company outside the Palace of Joy, Gregory homebound, Milhauser beginning a wary patrol of Main Street.

In the corridor outside Doc Corkhill's surgery meanwhile, the Texans paced and chain-smoked. They bared their heads and drawled friendly greetings when a wide-eyed and anxious Phoebe arrived. In his best big-brotherly manner, Larry wrapped a brawny arm about her trembling shoulders and offered comfort.

"Could be worse, Phoebe. Shoulder-wound. And you know Doc'll patch him right."

"He's suffering and — in pain," she sighed. "And so brave. Dad told me — he actually shielded him."

"That takes guts — beggin' your pardon," muttered Stretch.

The tall men were still attending the judge's daughter when, some time later, Doc opened the surgery door and beckoned them.

8

Killer Number 5 — Plus Three

THE patient could now be transferred to his quarters above his poky office on North Main. Not too risky a move, with the Texans acting as stretcher-bearers. Doc had removed the bullet without difficulty and applied a dressing which he would change tomorrow. Warren was conscious, but weak from loss of blood.

"He'll be asleep by the time you're putting him in his bed," the medico predicted. "Take heart, Phoebe love. A week or two will see him up and about. Of course, starting tomorrow, you'll need to build up his strength."

"She's good at that, Warren ol' buddy," Stretch assured the patient, while helping transfer him to the stretcher. "We ought to know, Larry and me."

"You won't look so scrawny," promised Larry, "after a couple weeks of Phoebe's cookin'."

"I'm causing — so much — trouble . . . " fretted Warren.

"How's that for modesty?" remarked Doc. "Twice he's saved Orin's life, and he thinks he's causing trouble."

"Be quiet, Warren dear," begged Phoebe. "Stay calm and don't worry about anything." As the Texans began toting the patient out, she moved along with them. "Carry him very carefully — please?"

Concerned townfolk made way for the tall men as, with Phoebe as their guide, they toted the hapless hero north along Main. Moving carefully, concentrating on their route, the Texans were oblivious to the tension in the atmosphere of the town.

To the locals, it seemed different, ominously so, to other payday Saturdays. Ranch-hands were in town in force, the morning was sunny and the sky clear, but the almost festive feeling just wasn't there. The cowboys were in bad humor, patronizing the saloons, sure, socializing with barkeeps and townmen, but mostly talking among themselves, and bitterly.

Warren was sleeping the sleep of utter exhaustion when the Texans laid him on his bed. Phoebe then fussed with the pillow, drew the covers up, lowered the window shade and wondered what else she could do. Larry gently assured her there was no other service she could perform for her hero at this time.

"And don't fret about fixin' his supper tonight," he advised, as they descended to Warren's cluttered office. "Leave that to Doc and us. Better you stay with your father."

"You can fetch his breakfast to-morrow," offered Stretch.

"What he needs most now is rest, Doc said," Larry reminded her. "Wouldn't make any difference you sittin' by his bed, holdin' his hand."

"I suppose you're right," she shrugged, when they reached the street. "And surely this is the end of it — or is it possible the fifth of those escapees could come to Alvison? Oh, Larry, it's like a nightmare — the bloodshed — the craving for vengeance against — a man like my father."

"Mightn't happen again," drawled Stretch.

"Don't fret about it anyway," said Larry. "We'll be around."

"You mean . . . ?" she frowned.

"Keepin' an eye on the house," he nodded. "Just in case."

"When Roy Dent returned to the Sentinel office, his all-purpose hired hand, the gruff-voiced, pipe-puffing Oley Barrow offered a prediction.

"It's gonna be a rough Saturday."

"Had your ear to the ground as usual, Oley?" Dent grinned wryly as he hung up his hat and coat. "Gleaning information from your reliable sources?"

"You want to know the mood of the town, you can't do better than listen to Burke the barber and O'Hare the barkeep," declared Barrow.

"Gossip-mongers," said Dent.

"You ever know 'em to be wrong?" challenged Barrow.

"Rarely," Dent admitted. "So what's the word? Why is every ranch-hand wearing an ugly frown instead of the usual payday grin?"

"They're turnin' mean," warned Barrow. "Now that they've learned how it started — that hullabaloo at the Palace — they're plenty leery of Rober and his people. If that big Texan caught Rober cheatin', why couldn't it have happened before? That's what they're sayin'. And wonderin' how much of their hard-earned coin was lost to a rigged game at the Palace"

"Let's hope their resentment doesn't flare to violence," frowned Dent. "Not that I've any respect for Rober. Anything else?"

"They're rememberin' Cleaver Moss is Rober's partner," said Barrow. "And it's for sure Melville parleyed with

Rober at the Palace before he went to the Blake house to settle his score with the judge."

"Which means Rober and an escaped killer weren't exactly strangers to each other," mused Dent.

"Somethin' else," said Barrow. "Must've been a dozen cowpokes saw Moss and Prince cut and run from Billy Bob Grebb. For a long time, our sheriff and his trigger-happy cousin been keepin' rowdy ranch-hands in line, but now everybody knows the truth about 'em. They're plain yellow, Roy. It had to be a puny shavetail lawyer tried to protect the judge against that killer, and it had to be Valentine put Grebb down. Not our gallant law officers. Just a scared young'un and a gun-smart drifter."

"So you could be right," said Dent. "You, Burke the barber and O'Hare the barkeep. This could be a bad Saturday."

Bad Saturday was an understatement, as subsequent events proved. By

3 o'clock that afternoon, Alvison's peace-loving citizenry were giving Main Street a wide berth, staying indoors and making sure their offspring did likewise. Better than 80 hard-drinking ranch-hands swaggered the main stem in incendiary mood while, in the law office, Moss and Prince sweated in apprehension. Milhauser was the only lawman out and about, trying to watch three areas simultaneously, the street and its northern and southern approaches. On the one hand, he hoped to dissuade the cowhands from violence. On the other hand, there had been no word of Cole Alton's recapture; he was not discounting the possibility of the fifth Blake-hater appearing on the scene.

By sundown, a score of more likkered-up cattlemen, backed by as many excitement-hungry townmen, were jamming the area in front of the Palace of Joy, filling the air with shouted profanity and wild threats. When the Texans viewed that ugly scene, only

Milhauser stood between the rioters and the saloon entrance. He had not drawn his gun. He was still attempting verbal dissuasion.

"We gonna do anything about this?" Stretch casually enquired.

"Tell you what," frowned Larry. "For starters, let's take a look around back."

"We were about to head for the Blake house," Stretch reminded him.

"Uh huh," grunted Larry. "So we'd best not waste too much time here."

Darting into the side alley, they hurried to the rear of the saloon to watch the hasty exit of Rober's hired women. The panic had begun, they realized. Only natural these bawds would be first to flee the threatened Palace. And one of Rober's tablemen followed them out through the back door and along the rear alley. They noted the firestairs leading up to a balcony and a lighted window.

"Think we'll find him up there?" prodded Stretch.

"We might." Larry grinned coldly. "We just might."

Climbing to the balcony, they checked the window. Unlocked. Rober loosed a startled gasp as they opened the window and clambered in to confront him. He was crouched by his safe, about to unlock it, his moon-face shiny with sweat. The clamor from the street was the most frightening sound he had ever heard — until that window opened.

"Don't I have trouble enough?" he cried, rising to berate them. "Not one paying customer in the barroom — just my hired hands to protect the palace from that crazy mob. And it's all your fault, Valentine!"

"Depends which way you look at it," Larry coolly countered.

"Somebody's got to do something!" wailed Rober. "If those hotheads break in, they'll wreck the place!" Suddenly inspired, he grinned eagerly and declared, "You jaspers could do it. Why sure! They know how tough you are. You're the hot-shots licked my whole staff. You could hold 'em back. Yeah! they'd listen to you!"

"I think he means it, runt," Stretch said in wonderment.

"Listen, name your price," urged Rober. "It's worth big money to me, having you faze those roughnecks away from here. How does a thousand sound? Not enough? All right, you got me over a barrel. Fifteen hundred I'm offering. Cash in hand right here and now."

"You that sure we can turn 'em back?" frowned Larry.

"I'm counting on you," Rober said impatiently. Come on now. How much is it gonna cost me?"

Larry's answer caused him to wince uneasily.

"Three hundred."

"Uh — well now — I'll admit we got off to a bad start, Valentine, but . . . "

"Three hundred," repeated Larry, poker faced.

"Yeah, sure, whatever you say," mumbled Rober, fishing out his wallet.

He extracted six $50 bills and dropped them on the desk. Larry gathered them up, stowed them in his own wallet and nodded curtly.

"Okay, open the door. We'll go down now."

Rober stumbled in his haste to reach the door and unlock it. The tall men moved out to the gallery and made for the stairs. They heard Rober's door closed and re-locked, and then the louder, crashing sound. From the gallery rail, they watched the beginning of the end of the Palace of Joy.

The cowhands had gained entry by rushing Milhauser and wrecking the street-door. Now, with Milhauser ahead of them, brandishing his Colt and demanding they stay orderly, fifteen of them surged in to be confronted by the only remaining employees. Big Anse, one barkeep and two table-men warily retreated to the rear wall.

"I like Dutch," said Stretch. "Whatever happens, I'd sure hate to see him hurt."

"Maybe they'll listen to us," shrugged Larry. "For a while anyway." They moved to the stairs and began their descent. Sighting and recognizing them, the rioters left off abusing the deputy and waited. Milhauser called to them urgently. "Louder, Dutch," drawled Larry. "What's that you're sayin'?"

"I'm sayin' I can't close up the place," growled Milhauser. "That's what they want, but I can't do it."

"Why?" Larry mildly challenged. "Seems like a good idea to me, Dutch."

"To hang a closed sign out front, I'd have to be able to prove Rober's been cheatin' 'em," explained Milhauser.

"You got to admit that's reasonable, runt," said Stretch.

"Real reasonable," agreed Larry. He nodded affably to the eager-for-action ranch-hands. "So, if you bucks'll give me and my partner a couple minutes to do a little checkin' . . ."

Milhauser was plagued by uncertainty, but striving to maintain a stern, purposeful exterior, when the Texans began moving among the gaming tables, the cowhands watching intently.

At a poker table, Larry picked up a sealed deck, tore the wrapper and inspected a few cards. He grimaced in disgust and moved on to the roulette table, while Stretch positioned himself at the dice table. After tossing dice for a couple of moments, he placed two on an index finger as though testing their weight. He tossed them again, shook his head sadly and drawled,

"What d'you know? Them bones is loaded."

"Just like Shorty said!" raged a cowpoke. "It's a gyp-joint."

"Quiet, everybody!" ordered Milhauser. When Larry overturned the roulette-table to inspect its mechanism, the supervisor made to move forward.

"You won't find . . . " he began.

"Stay back," growled Milhauser. "Well, Valentine, what d'you say?"

Larry left the roulette table on its side, frowned accusingly at the supervisor and told the deputy,

"You'd best shut 'em down."

"All right, that's it, boys!" Milhauser raised his voice above the profanity of the cowhands. "All move out! The Palace is closed until further notice!"

But the uproar continued after the hotheads quit the building. And, as the Texans departed by way of the rear exit, Rober's employees traded worried glances. There was only one thought in their minds now. Feeling was running high against Rober. Very soon, the fury of a hundred sore losers would rise to fever-pitch and there was no way Milhauser could hold them back. So to stay on there seemed downright foolhardy.

From Main Street, the Texans hurried to the Blake house. They were admitted by Phoebe who, at Larry's request, conducted them to the parlor to speak with her father. Blake, still brooding on recent bloody events, reacted bitterly to the Texans' offer.

"It's come to this?" he scowled. "The

law officers of this county are suddenly incapable of protecting a cripple? I'm to rely on — men I barely know turning my home into a fortress?"

"Dutch Milhauser ain't hidin', Judge," Stretch assured him. "He's on the job and ready to do his duty."

"But Dutch is only one man," muttered Larry. "Look, Judge, we don't mean to take over your home. I only wanted you to know we'll be around — real close — if we're needed." He nodded to Phoebe. "Mightn't be anything happen anyway. You just keep the doors and windows locked and, if anybody comes visitin', you don't let 'em in 'less you recognize their voice, savvy?"

"No strangers," she grimly promised. "I'll never make that mistake again, Larry."

"You don't have to worry about us gettin' in your way," Larry told Blake. "We'll be outside. But close."

"You intend keeping my home under surveillance?" demanded Blake.

"Thunderation! For how long, may I ask?"

"I reckon you know the answer to that question," said Larry.

"Tomorrow, for instance," offered Stretch. "If the telegrapher gets the word on this Horton hombre . . . "

"Alton," corrected Blake. "Cole Alton."

"Well, if he gets word some search party nailed Alton, why, me and Larry'll just tell you adios and ride right out of this town," declared Stretch. "And then you'll be rid of us."

"Rid of you." Blake sighed heavily. "Gentlemen, forgive my harsh reaction to your well-meant offer. I could hardly wish to be rid of men who've twice saved my life."

"So just don't fret about it, okay?" urged Larry. "Read your newspaper, fix yourself a drink, smoke a cigar. And just remember we'll be around."

"Which means no jasper's gonna get close enough to do you a harm," nodded Stretch.

A short time later, settling down to their vigil on the front porch, the trouble-shooters cocked ears to the sounds reaching them from the heart of town. They stared toward the corner of Mailey and Main and traded comments.

"Them waddies from the county spreads — runnin' wild," guessed Stretch.

"I ain't objectin'," growled Larry. "The way it seems to me, no regular citizen got anything to fear from 'em. I'm bettin' they're — uh ... " He grinned mirthlessly, "kind of concentratin' on Rober's place."

They were content to flop on that front porch indefinitely. Surveying their immediate surroundings, they assured themselves they would have fair warning of the approach of a marauder. There was a street-lamp opposite the house, another a short distance down Mailey, another illuminating the corner area.

When, from the general location of

the Palace of Joy, they saw flame and smoke rising to the night sky, they accurately concluded Rober's old customers were putting him out of business.

That was only the half of it. When, at 8.15 p.m., the four strangers entered Main Street from the south, the ranch-hands were still rioting, the Palace of Joy was well and truly afire, Deputy Milhauser trying to organize volunteer firefighters, Roy Dent dashing back and forth, gathering material for a report of the outbreak, and three men being tied to rails; Rober, Moss and Prince were about to be run out of town. Anticipating this, Rober's employees had departed an hour before.

"What I call quite a welcome," grinned Pinchon.

"Damn it, Cole!" breathed Craig. "Those men being carried away — tied to rails — two of them are lawmen. I saw their badges!"

"I saw 'em too," shrugged Martell. "And will you look at that place burn?"

"I didn't count on this fracas," drawled Alton. "But, since it's happening anyway, we can use it. Mighty handy, huh Carl? Perfect diversion?"

"You got a point," frowned Craig.

"Just leave this to me," ordered Alton. "I'll handle the talking."

He wheeled his mount to lead his companions to the excited group of townmen on the east sidewalk. For only a few moments, but only enough for one local to warily appraise him, he was caught in the light of a street-lamp. Roy Dent kept his eyes on the strangers as he edged closer to the townmen.

Alton addressed the locals sternly.

"Can none of your leading citizens put a stop to this rowdiness? Doesn't my friend Judge Blake know what's happening?"

"I don't reckon anything can be done," mumbled an old timer. "I don't know where the other deputy is. And — doggone it — the sheriff and Deputy Prince are gettin' run out on a rail."

"I refuse to believe Orin Blake would

ignore such an emergency," said Alton. "I'll appeal to him at once. Kindly direct me to his home."

"On Mailey Street," offered another man. "Double-storied place a little way along Mailey. White picket fence."

"First double-storied place from the corner this end," said the old timer, pointing. "You can't miss it."

"Thank you," nodded Alton. "Come, gentlemen. This outrage must be brought to Orin's attention without further delay."

Nerves a'clamor, Dent scurried away in search of the Texans, a search doomed to failure.

'I could be wrong,' he reflected, as he reached the fringe of the crowd watching the fiery destructiopn of the Palace. 'But — if I'm right . . . ?'

When the harassed Deputy Milhauser emerged from the crowd, Dent hurried to him and confide his suspicions.

"He's on his way to Orin's home, Dutch. And the hell of it is — he's not alone! There are four of them!"

"Could be Alton, you think?" challenged Milhauser.

"This man isn't bearded, but the resemblance . . . "

"All right, Mister Dent. Thanks for lettin' me know."

"Dutch, you'll need help. You can't go up against all four of them. Give me time to find Valentine and Emerson."

"Got to head for Mailey Street rightaway," Milhauser said firmly. "Look for Valentine and his partner if you want, but I can't wait."

When the four riders turned their horses off Main and entered Mailey, the Texans sat up and took notice. The advance was slow, almost casual, but they weren't about to take chances. Descending from the porch, hugging shrubbery and shadowy areas, they began working their way to the picket fence.

Almost opposite the house, the strangers began drawing rein. And, at that moment, Milhauser hustled around the corner from the main

246

street, sighted them and called his challenge.

"You men down there! Identify yourselves!"

Glancing over his shoulder, Martell chuckled softly and announced,

"He wears a law-badge. I can see it clear."

"Me too," grinned Pinchon. "Makes a right fine target."

He drew and fired while still mounted and, nearing the fence, Larry darted a glance toward the corner and cursed explosively. Milhauser had drawn, but was staggering drunkenly, going down.

"Let's get it over with," scowled Alton, as he swung down. The other three followed his example. And then, squaring his shoulders, he began crossing toward the house with his cohorts at his heels. "Blake!" he called loudly. "This is Cole Alton! Come out and face me! If I have to go in there for you . . ."

"That's as far as you're comin', jailbird!" growled Larry. With that, he vaulted the fence. "Hold it right there!"

Dropping to the boardwalk a few yards to Larry's right, Stretch added his own warning.

"It's been tried — by four other runaways — and now they're six feet under."

"Blake stays alive," Larry said harshly.

The four jerked to a halt, intently studying their challengers. Along the street, near the corner, a local quit his home and hurried across to where the stricken deputy lay sprawled. Alton and his cronies heard the footsteps, but didn't shift their gaze from the tall men on the opposite sidewalk. Pinchon, hefting his smoking Colt, leering in unholy anticipation.

"I'll warn you heroes just this once," snapped Alton. "Try standing between me and Blake and you'll end up as dead as I intend him to be."

"Makes quite a speech, don't he, runt?" remarked Stretch. "Talks real fancy — for a jailbird."

"I'm Cole Alton!" snarled Alton. "If you've heard of me, you know you don't stand a chance!"

"I'm Valentine — he's Emerson," offered Larry. "if you ain't heard of us, we don't care a damn."

"But make it easy on yourself," advised Stretch. "Tell your buddy with the gun to drop it. The rest of you unstrap your hardware."

"By Judas, Cole!" breathed Pinchon. "They're beggin' for it!"

As his Colt roared, Alton, Craig and Martell swiftly emptied their holsters, but no faster than the Texans drew and fired. Stretch's left hand .45 boomed as Pinchon's bullet creased him. He lurched sideways with his other gun working and, as he began falling, had the grim satisfaction of seeing Pinchon reel, of hearing his cry of agony.

The street vibrated to the thunder of gunfire now. Larry had beaten Alton's draw and was triggering and re-cocking and triggering again, watching Alton fall and writhe and Craig backstepping with his gun blazing. He fired again and, as though struck by a giant fist, Craig spun wildly and crashed to the dust. Something that felt like a red-hot running iron filled Larry's torso with fiery pain and started his senses reeling. His legs gave way under him and he began falling and, chuckling triumphantly, the as yet unscathed Martell drew another bead on him and re-cocked.

To the consternation of the man hovering over him, Milhauser bellowed a curse, rolled onto his left side and raised his Colt.

"You're covered!" he cried. "Drop it or I fire!"

Martell chuckled again and yelled a taunt.

"From that far off — you couldn't hit a barn wall! I'll take care of you — after I finish off these no-accounts!"

Gritting his teeth, Milhauser thrust his right arm forward and fired. Martell flinched and began turning toward him as that first bullet swished past his face. He re-cocked and fired again and, awe-struck, the man crouched beside the prone deputy watched Martell jerk convulsively, drop his gun and paw at his chest. The half-breed loosed a strident wail, flopped to his knees, pitched forward with his face in the dust and became as still as his dead cohorts.

"Fetch — doctor . . . " Milhauser mumbled to the local. "*Both* doctors! Damn it, mister, don't just stand there gawkin'!" Hampered by his leg-wound, he twisted to glare up at the man. His jaw sagged. "Sonofagun! If it ain't — Mister Ellis . . . !"

Luther Ellis, manager of the Settlers Trust Bank, nodded soberly.

"Yes, Deputy Milhauser. And, if you'll permit me to help you to the sidewalk, I'll be only too glad to summon the doctors. That's the least I can do — for a lawman of such courage and fortitude."

"Courage and fortitude, huh?" The deputy grinned coldly as the banker helped him to his feet. "As I recall, that ain't what you said about me — after them smart thieves emptied your safe."

"Do you mind if I postpone the apology I owe you?" begged Ellis. "I'll need time to rehearse it."

"I don't need no speech," mumbled Milhauser.

"The hell you don't," sighed Ellis. "Beg pardon would hardly seem adequate."

* * *

Daylight was streaming through the window of the double room at the Guyatt Hotel when Larry next opened his eyes. Grunting, he worked himself a little higher on his pillows and gingerly felt at the right side of his heavily-bandaged torso. Then his vision began clearing. He heard voices close at hand, the voices of three men. All three voices were familiar to him, one more so than the others. And, for this, he was profoundly grateful.

"Both of us nicked in the same place — can you beat that?" Stretch was remarking to Judge Blake and Roy Dent. "Only — uh — my ol' buddy Larry just got to do everything the hard way, so his crease is some deeper'n mine."

"Valentine's awake," observed Dent. "Valentine, how do you feel?" He grinned apologetically. "Sorry. That was a dumb question."

"You didn't — sound so dumb . . . " mumbled Larry. "Before, I mean. Talkin' up for the beanpole and me — at the trial . . . "

"No obligation," shrugged Dent. "I'm not asking for an interview. It's a little late anyway. I have a special edition circulating already."

"The Bormann authorities have been advised, Mister Valentine," offered Blake. "The last of the five will be buried this afternoon — with his accomplices."

"Five killers who should have paid

the supreme penalty years ago, Orin," said Dent. "So what price capital punishment now, old friend?"

"Let's debate that question at a later date," suggested Blake. "Before Phoebe arrives to serve our friends a meal, I think we should satisfy their curiosity. Then they may relax."

"Hey, runt, they already told me somethin'," drawled Stretch.

"Such as?" prodded Larry.

"Such as we're plumb lucky to be alive," declared Stretch. "Seems I only downed one of them killers before I flopped. You got two — and then *you* flopped. That left one of 'em still in business and, if it wasn't for Dutch, he'd have finished us off."

"Dutch was down with a leg-wound," Dent told Larry. "And who do you suppose came running out of his home at that moment? Luther Ellis, manager of the Settlers Trust and, until now, Dutch's loudest critic."

"Luther could only stand and watch," said Blake, "when Deputy Milhauser

254

accounted for the fourth gunman."

"Before that fourth gunman could account for you and your partner," nodded Dent.

"That's one we owe Dutch," Larry wearily declared.

"Soon as we're on our feet," agreed Stretch.

"You'll be laid up a week at least, according to Phin Corkhill," said Dent.

"How about Dutch's leg?" demanded Larry.

"He's Doc Howland's patient," said Dent. "Dutch took a bullet in his right thigh. Young Howland has removed the slug and done everything a surgeon could hope to do, but we're told Dutch will never regain the full use of that leg."

"Rough," sighed Larry.

"So he's through as a lawman," guessed Stretch.

"No, by golly," grinned Dent.

"We've been in conference with Mayor Grove and the town council," explained Blake. "As you'll appreciate, the expulsion of Cleaver Moss, Jesse Prince and Neeley Rober leaves us with an emergency situation on our hands."

"Expulsion is putting it politely," Dent said with grim relish. "They ran 'em out on a rail. And the Palace of Joy was burnt to the ground."

"What I call a real emergency, Judge," remarked Larry. "Two lawmen gone. Only one deputy left, and him laid up with a leg-wound."

"At the jailhouse, Jug must be powerful lonely," frowned Stretch.

"The council voted to have Mayor Grove's nephew come to Alvison to take over as sheriff," said Blake.

"Good man with ample experience," said Dent. "Deputy-marshal of some North Colorado town. He'll be here in a few days."

"Prince will have to be replaced, of course," Blake went on. "But it was unanimously agreed Milhauser's services should be retained."

"As chief deputy," grinned Dent.

"Sounds impressive, huh? Luther Ellis is on the council, you see, and he insisted Dutch is too good a lawman to lose, even if he has to use a cane the rest of his life."

"Phoebe should arrive any time now," opined the judge, after checking his watch. "Roy, can you think of anything we've neglected to mention?"

"They're probably wondering about young Kipp," suggested Dent.

"Yeah, how about the kid-lawyer?" asked Stretch.

"Making satisfactory progress, Phin says," offered Blake. "He looked in on Warren after treating your wounds. Yes, my future son-in-law should make a slow but sure recovery."

"Future son-in-law?" Larry grinned approvingly. "What'd he do? Propose to Phoebe next time he came to his senses?"

"I think he'd come to his senses, but was in no condition to propose," smiled Blake. "So Phoebe proposed. My daughter can be unconventional at times, but she knows what she wants."

"Couldn't happen to two nicer young folks," enthused Larry.

"Ain't that the truth," agreed Stretch.

Eight days later, stiff and sore, but mobile again, the Texans checked out of the hotel, stopped by a general store for necessary supplies, then carried their gear and their purchases to the stable where their animals were quartered. It was time for them to shake the dust of Alvison off their boots, the later stages of their convalescence having been aggravated by an old and incurable irritation very familiar to them — itchy feet. What more could they do for themselves or for Alvison? Order had been restored by the new sheriff and his junior deputy, an ambitious 22-year-old recruited from one of the local ranches.

En route to the barn, they paused to study the activity in the area once occupied by Alvison's biggest saloon and gambling house; workmen were clearing the site of blackened rubble in preparation for the construction of a new building.

"Some would say Rober paid a heavy price for dealin' himself an ace from under," Stretch remarked. "Three hundred he took us for. And what'd it cost him? The whole shebang. All his hired help spooked and quit and he got run out on a rail, him and cousin Jesse and ol' Big-Gut Moss."

"I call it even," growled Larry. "The hell with Rober and all his kind. With me, a cardsharp rates no higher than a horsethief, a brand-changer or a back-shooter."

They moved on to the stable, paid for feed and board of the sorrel and pinto and readied them for the trail. Double cinches secured, Winchesters sheathed, saddlebags full and packrolls lashed into position, they led their mounts into Main Street, raised boots to stirrups and swung astride gratefully — because their most recent shootout might well have been their last. It was cause for sober reflection, the fact that a homicidal adversary could have emptied a Colt into them while they lay semi-conscious and helpless, but for the fighting spirit and keen eye of the deputy Alvison had despised.

For Milhauser, the bad days were past. The Texans had plied him with good whiskey at a downtown saloon yesterday afternoon and it had been all too clear that Alvison men were eager to make amends. Not only had the proprietor and barkeep accorded Milhauser respect and friendliness; so had every other customer.

When they drew rein in front of the law office, Chief-Deputy Milhauser was resting on the porch, his cane leaning against his chair, his expression mellow. Doc Corkhill had stopped by to visit and was perched on the porch-rail.

Before either Texan could drawl a greeting, Doc got in the first word.

"I've decided it *is* the Texas climate,"

he announced. "You bucks are the tallest I ever met, so that clinches it. When I get around to writing my treatise on the subject, I intend devoting several pages to the relationship between climatic environment and development of physical attributes."

"Ain't sure what that all means, Doc," grinned Stretch. "But it sounds real polite."

"Dutch, how're you feelin'?" asked Larry.

"Better every day," nodded Milhauser. "You two?"

"We'll make out," shrugged Stretch. "We heal fast."

"That's no idle brag," Doc assured the deputy. "While I was patching their wounds, I was tempted to count the scars on their leathery hides. Gave up on the idea. Couldn't spare the time it would take." Good-humoredly, he enquired, "What else do you nomads do besides getting shot at?"

"You mean you ain't guessed, Doc?" Larry grinned ruefully. "We try stayin'

261

out of trouble — so we *won't* get shot at."

"Thanks again, Dutch," offered Stretch. "We ain't forgettin' what you did for us."

"Well, you and young Kipp'd been cheatin' me all along," drawled Milhauser. "I had to get at least *one* shot at a killer."

"You made it count," declared Larry. "And that's why we're still alive." He raised a hand in farewell. "All the luck, Dutch. You too, Doc."

"Hold it," begged Milhauser. "Somethin' I'm curious about. You just got to tell me before you leave, else I'll never know."

"Sure," nodded Larry. "What d'you want to know?"

"In the Palace, when you and Stretch checked Rober's games of chance — the poker deck, the wheel, the dice?" Milhauser eyed them intently. "You sure the deck was marked, the roulette rigged, the dice loaded?"

The drifters traded blank stares.

"Well," said Stretch. "Them dice *could've* been loaded."

"I looked under the wheel," Larry recalled. "But what would *I* know? What am I — an engineer?"

Milhauser swore softly.

"You mean — you weren't sure at all?"

"Who can be sure of anything?" Doc idly wondered. "It's an uncertain world, Dutch."

"Don't fret about it, Dutch," advised Larry, as he nudged the sorrel to movement. "Adios, amigo. You too, Doc."

"If we ever stop by Alvison again — which ain't likely — we'll be sure and look you up," promised Stretch.

"Two very special men," remarked Doc, watching the Texans ride south along Main. "But restless. Men of no purpose. So what's to become of them?"

"They don't need for you to worry about 'em, Doc," opined Milhauser. "Better you should fret for the next bunch of killers they tangle with."

"Nine new graves in our cemetery — Larry and Stretch still on the move," mused Doc. "You're right, Dutch. They're a couple of survivors. And, in this town, they'll not be forgotten."

"Not anyplace else," Milhauser predicted.

THE END

Books by Marshall Grover
in the Linford Western Library:

CALABOOSE EXPRESS
WHISKEY GULCH
THE ALIBI TRAIL
SIX GUILTY MEN
FORT DILLON
IN PURSUIT OF QUINCEY BUDD
HAMMER'S HORDE
TWO GENTLEMEN FROM TEXAS
HARRIGAN'S STAR
TURN THE KEY ON EMERSON
ROUGH ROUTE TO RODD COUNTY
SEVEN KILLERS EAST
DAKOTA DEATH-TRAP
GOLD, GUNS AND THE GIRL
RUCKUS AT GILA WELLS
LEGEND OF COYOTE FORD
ONE HELL OF A SHOWDOWN
EMERSON'S HEX
SIX GUN WEDDING
THE GOLD MOVERS
WILD NIGHT IN WIDOW'S PEAK
THE TINHORN MURDER CASE
TERROR FOR SALE
HOSTAGE HUNTERS
WILD WIDOW OF WOLF CREEK
THE LAWMAN WORE BLACK

THE DUDE MUST DIE
WAIT FOR THE JUDGE
HOLD 'EM BACK!
WELLS FARGO DECOYS
WE RIDE FOR CIRCLE 6
THE CANNON MOUND GANG

Other titles in the
Linford Western Library:

TOP HAND
Wade Everett

The Broken T was big. But no ranch is big enough to let a man hide from himself.

GUN WOLVES OF LOBO BASIN
Lee Floren

The Feud was a blood debt. When Smoke Talbot found the outlaws who gunned down his folks he aimed to nail their hide to the barn door.

SHOTGUN SHARKEY
Marshall Grover

The westbound coach carrying the indomitable Larry and Stretch headed for a shooting showdown.

FIGHTING RAMROD
Charles N. Heckelmann

Most men would have cut their losses, but Frazer counted the bullets in his guns and said he'd soak the range in blood before he'd give up another inch of what was his.

LONE GUN
Eric Allen

Smoke Blackbird had been away too long. The Lequires had seized the Blackbird farm, forcing the Indians and settlers off, and no one seemed willing to fight! He had to fight alone.

THE THIRD RIDER
Barry Cord

Mel Rawlins wasn't going to let anything stand in his way. His father was murdered, his two brothers gone. Now Mel rode for vengeance.

ARIZONA DRIFTERS
W. C. Tuttle

When drifting Dutton and Lonnie Steelman decide to become partners they find that they have a common enemy in the formidable Thurston brothers.

TOMBSTONE
Matt Braun

Wells Fargo paid Luke Starbuck to outgun the silver-thieving stagecoach gang at Tombstone. Before long Luke can see the only thing bearing fruit in this eldorado will be the gallows tree.

HIGH BORDER RIDERS
Lee Floren

Buckshot McKee and Tortilla Joe cut the trail of a border tough who was running Mexican beef into Texas. They stopped the smuggler in his tracks.

BRETT RANDALL, GAMBLER
E. B. Mann

Larry Day had the choice of running away from the law or of assuming a dead man's place. No matter what he decided he was bound to end up dead.

THE GUNSHARP
William R. Cox

The Eggerleys weren't very smart. They trained their sights on Will Carney and Arizona's biggest blood bath began.

THE DEPUTY OF SAN RIANO
Lawrence A. Keating and
Al. P. Nelson

When a man fell dead from his horse, Ed Grant was spotted riding away from the scene. The deputy sheriff rode out after him and came up against everything from gunfire to dynamite.

FARGO: MASSACRE RIVER
John Benteen

The ambushers up ahead had now blocked the road. Fargo's convoy was a jumble, a perfect target for the insurgents' weapons!

SUNDANCE: DEATH IN THE LAVA
John Benteen

The Modoc's captured the wagon train and its cargo of gold. But now the halfbreed they called Sundance was going after it . . .

HARSH RECKONING
Phil Ketchum

Five years of keeping himself alive in a brutal prison had made Brand tough and careless about who he gunned down . . .

FARGO: PANAMA GOLD
John Benteen

With foreign money behind him, Buckner was going to destroy the Panama Canal before it could be completed. Fargo's job was to stop Buckner.

FARGO:
THE SHARPSHOOTERS
John Benteen

The Canfield clan, thirty strong were raising hell in Texas. Fargo was tough enough to hold his own against the whole clan.

PISTOL LAW
Paul Evan Lehman

Lance Jones came back to Mustang for just one thing — revenge! Revenge on the people who had him thrown in jail.

HELL RIDERS
Steve Mensing

Wade Walker's kid brother, Duane, was locked up in the Silver City jail facing a rope at dawn. Wade was a ruthless outlaw, but he was smart, and he had vowed to have his brother out of jail before morning!

DESERT OF THE DAMNED
Nelson Nye

The law was after him for the murder of a marshal — a murder he didn't commit. Breen was after him for revenge — and Breen wouldn't stop at anything . . . blackmail, a frameup . . . or murder.

DAY OF THE COMANCHEROS
Steven C. Lawrence

Their very name struck terror into men's hearts — the Comancheros, a savage army of cutthroats who swept across Texas, leaving behind a bloodstained trail of robbery and murder.

SUNDANCE: SILENT ENEMY
John Benteen

A lone crazed Cheyenne was on a personal war path. They needed to pit one man against one crazed Indian. That man was Sundance.

LASSITER
Jack Slade

Lassiter wasn't the kind of man to listen to reason. Cross him once and he'll hold a grudge for years to come — if he let you live that long.

LAST STAGE TO GOMORRAH
Barry Cord

Jeff Carter, tough ex-riverboat gambler, now had himself a horse ranch that kept him free from gunfights and card games. Until Sturvesant of Wells Fargo showed up.

McALLISTER ON THE COMANCHE CROSSING
Matt Chisholm

The Comanche, McAllister owes them a life — and the trail is soaked with the blood of the men who had tried to outrun them before.

QUICK-TRIGGER COUNTRY
Clem Colt

Turkey Red hooked up with Curly Bill Graham's outlaw crew. But wholesale murder was out of Turk's line, so when range war flared he bucked the whole border gang alone . . .

CAMPAIGNING
Jim Miller

Ambushed on the Santa Fe trail, Sean Callahan is saved by two Indian strangers. But there'll be more lead and arrows flying before the band join Kit Carson against the Comanches.

GUNSLINGER'S RANGE
Jackson Cole

Three escaped convicts are out for revenge. They won't rest until they put a bullet through the head of the dirty snake who locked them behind bars.

RUSTLER'S TRAIL
Lee Floren

Jim Carlin knew he would have to stand up and fight because he had staked his claim right in the middle of Big Ike Outland's best grass.

THE TRUTH ABOUT SNAKE RIDGE
Marshall Grover

The troubleshooters came to San Cristobal to help the needy. For Larry and Stretch the turmoil began with a brawl and then an ambush.

WOLF DOG RANGE
Lee Floren

Will Ardery would stop at nothing, unless something stopped him first — like a bullet from Pete Manly's gun.

DEVIL'S DINERO
Marshall Grover

Plagued by remorse, a rich old reprobate hired the Texas Trouble-shooters to deliver a fortune in greenbacks to each of his victims.

GUNS OF FURY
Ernest Haycox

Dane Starr, alias Dan Smith, wanted to close the door on his past and hang up his guns, but people wouldn't let him.

DONOVAN
Elmer Kelton

Donovan was supposed to be dead. Uncle Joe Vickers had fired off both barrels of a shotgun into the vicious outlaw's face as he was escaping from jail. Now Uncle Joe had been shot — in just the same way.

CODE OF THE GUN
Gordon D. Shirreffs

MacLean came riding home, with saddle tramp written all over him, but sewn in his shirt-lining was an Arizona Ranger's star.

GAMBLER'S GUN LUCK
Brett Austen

Gamblers seldom live long. Parker was a hell of a gambler. It was his life — or his death . . .

ORPHAN'S PREFERRED
Jim Miller

Sean Callahan answers the call of the Pony Express and fights Indians and outlaws to get the mail through.

DAY OF THE BUZZARD
T. V. Olsen

All Val Penmark cared about was getting the men who killed his wife.

THE MANHUNTER
Gordon D. Shirreffs

Lee Kershaw knew that every Rurale in the territory was on the lookout for him. But the offer of $5,000 in gold to find five small pieces of leather was too good to turn down.

RIFLES ON THE RANGE
Lee Floren

Doc Mike and the farmer stood there alone between Smith and Watson. There was this moment of stillness, and then the roar would start. And somebody would die . . .

HARTIGAN
Marshall Grover

Hartigan had come to Cornerstone to die. He chose the time and the place, and Main Street became a battlefield.

SUNDANCE: OVERKILL
John Benteen

When a wealthy banker's daughter was kidnapped by the Cheyenne, he offered Sundance $10,000 to rescue the girl.

RIDE A LONE TRAIL
Gordon D. Shirreffs

The valley was about to explode into open range war. All it needed was the fuse and Ken Macklin was it.

HARD MAN WITH A GUN
Charles N. Heckelmann

After Bob Keegan lost the girl he loved and the ranch he had sweated blood to build, he had nothing left but his guts and his guns but he figured that was enough.

SUNDANCE: IRON MEN
Peter McCurtin

Sundance, assigned to save the railroad from a murder spree, soon came to realise that he'd have to fight fire with fire, bullets with bullets and death with death!